MAD茱莉的文法冒險

大石健
Miguel Rivas-Micoud 著
本局編輯部譯

三民書局

給讀者的話

你是否覺得這是本奇怪的文法書呢？這是有理由的。

首先，一旦開口說英語，不知為何老是犯同樣的錯；別難過，這不是你個人的問題，應該說是英語和中文在「文法」上的差異使然吧！本書共分 80 個單元，每篇都是以這些人們常犯的錯誤作探討，當中也有不少單元看似簡單，其實也真的很簡單，但是你不見得都會。不信嗎？試試看便知。

第二個理由是，拿「文法」當 rule 死背的結果只有一條——此路不通。此話怎講？文法的使用必須是在具體的狀況下（也就是在情境當中），當說話者以感情、意念等自發性的積極姿態和對方 communicate 時才得以成立；換句話說，就是英語的「文法」必須內化為中文使用者的一部分，因為只有當文法使用得不著痕跡，它才真正屬於你。

這也是為什麼我們試著將 80 個單元串成故事，不像其他書籍以刻板人物、定型場景作文章，我們設計了茉莉 (Mari) 這樣一號人物，藉由她不時發出的「另類對話」挑戰讀者的神經，也帶領讀者一同進入她的故事，共同感受英語的生命力。「想到什麼說什麼」其實不是茉莉的專利，而是人類通用的說話模式。仔細想想，你知道你下句話要說什麼嗎？沒錯，得說了才知道。語言是用來溝通，表達自己的情感，是用來輔助人類行為的，而臨場反應是對話中很重要的一環。

基於以上原因，本書並不想自我定位成一本講解錯誤文法的冊子，因為如果是這樣，其他書籍可能會做得更好。這本書是企圖模擬一個說中文的「我」，當他試圖透過英語表現自己、和別人溝通時，可能會有詞不達意，或甚至產生誤解的情形，這些錯誤都透過茉莉來讓讀者感同身受，進而內省、修正自己說英語的模式。其中的 Examples 及Notes 只是用來幫助理解，當你能忘掉 Notes 的內容，自自然然地說英語時，恭喜你，這表示你真的進步了。 Good luck and enjoy yourself!

P.S.

標題 MAD 茉莉中的 MAD 意思是茉莉是個有主見，不一味順從社會規範的人，跟小寫的 mad「瘋狂、魯莽、難纏」不同，大寫的 MAD 是個只屬於茉莉個人專用的榮譽稱謂。

關於「錯誤例句」的標示方法

各單元的標題皆為正確的英語，內文中以中空印刷的文字部分表示該處的英語文法錯誤，或是說法與當時的情境不符。

和標題無關的錯誤在內文中加注 * 符號，訂正後的正確說法則提示於該頁下方的注腳處。

譯句處理原則以正確性為主，不管茉莉的說法對或錯，譯句中所出現的均為茉莉原本想表達的語意，後方〔　〕內的部分則是對方誤以為茉莉想要表達的錯誤語意。

當茉莉的說法錯得太離譜時，便不特別以〔　〕加注錯誤的語意翻譯。

譯者的話

既要牽就原文又要譯得沒有外國腔，翻譯可以說是件吃力不討好的事。許多人以為翻譯沒有原創性，不過是鸚鵡學舌，照本宣科而已，但事實真的如此嗎？我很懷疑。

舉例來說， this（這）is（是）a（一本）book（書），直譯起來是一個蘿蔔一個坑，沒有問題，但是不同語言之間類似這種對號入座的句子畢竟可遇而不可求。

某人向你介紹他的女朋友，你衷心（或客套）地說了句 You are beautiful.〔你很漂亮〕，這時相信不會有人把它譯成〔你是漂亮的〕，因為這不像中文（的文法）；可是話又說回來，整句加起來一共三個字，其中沒有一個是代表「很漂亮」的「很」字，也就是英文裡像是 very 的字眼，按理說尊重原文的話，這時應該要把「很」字去掉，但是這麼一來如何翻譯可就得傷腦筋了。不合文法的英語我們稱之為洋涇濱英語，但是為什麼人們會說出貽笑大方的洋涇濱英語呢？原因和我們不自覺地將母語文法直接套用在外文上的下意識行為有關。同樣的道理，若是堅持尊重原文，一味依據外文的語法去作翻譯，結果便是滿嘴洋腔洋調的中文，怪異極了。因此我們不妨這麼說，當不同的語言在作轉換時，適當的添加及刪減絕對是少不了的「必要之惡」。

再舉一個例子，第 56 個單元的 will be～ing 未來進行式和第 60個單元的 will have been/～ed 未來完成式兩者在譯成中文後其實很不容易分辨。比方說前者強調在未來的某個時刻正在做～，後者則是（從現在起）到未來的某個時刻～將已經完結，本書中將兩項都譯成屆時就（已經），很明顯地前者不太對勁。因為如果採用直譯的方式： This time in May, I'll be lying on the beach! 的意思應該是〔到 5 月此時，我將正躺在沙灘上〕——這是句中文沒錯，但不可否認不怎麼自然。原因是中文很少有強調〔在未來的某個時刻我正在做～〕的未來進行式句型，反倒是〔到了 5 月此時，我就可以躺在沙灘上了〕之類強調屆時願望將會實現的句型比較常見，將後者反譯成英文後我們得到：This time in May, I'll lie on the beach! 但令人苦惱的是，「正在」跟「就可以／將」一個是已經實現，一個是將要開始，兩者所傳達的語感不盡相同。思考再思考後，譯者決定用「已經」這個帶有完成語氣的字眼，原因之一是它可以傳達出動作已經實現的語感；另一方面則是實現後的動作不管是正在進行／持續中，還是已經終止，就中文的特性來說，其實都不列入考慮（亦即沒有什麼差別）。

「信達雅」向來被視為是翻譯的最高境界，從分寸的拿捏可以看出大譯者和小譯者的功力差別。譯者的天職雖然是忠於原文，然而現實卻是不得不加以自由裁量，是該增還是該刪？又該增刪多少才算合理？一篇原文十個人來翻譯版本就有十個，所以結論還是讀者最好自己學著看原文，順便譯譯看，測試一下自己的理解程度。信不信由你，很多的文法概念其實透過外文和母語的對譯反而會更加地清晰。

在第一個單元中登場的麥克後來和茱莉發展出非常微妙的關係，而在第七單元一開頭向茱莉打招呼的約翰其實是接待家庭的男主人——史密斯先生，希望讀者別誤以為他是哪裡冒出來的登徒子。另外像是 OK，Oh，Ah，Umm 等語助詞的譯法，也是視當時情境而各有不同，至於箇中巧妙，就有待各位讀者自己慢慢體會了。

MAD 茱莉的文法冒險

目　次

[illegible]

There will be a meeting this Thursday.

[illegible]

Can you speak louder, please?

[illegible]

[illegible]

[illegible]

[illegible]

[illegible]

[illegible]

[illegible]

The more dangerous it is, the more I like it.

很久很久以前，

在美國的某個地方，

有個女孩名叫茉莉……

I

你有沒有兄弟姊妹？

Do you have any brothers or sisters?

Mike: You must be Mari Wang.

Mari: **Yes, that's right, but who are you?**

Mike: I'm Mike Bell. We're both in Drama 101.

Mari: **Oh, yes, I think I've seen you before.**

Mike: I always sit in the front.

Mari: **I'm *too shy, so I sit at the back.**

Mike: I'm from Key West.

Mari: **I don't know it.**

Mike: You should visit someday, it's beautiful.

Mari: **Do you have** brothers or sisters?

Mike: Uhh...yes, actually I do. Why?

Mari: **I am *a lonely child.**

Mike: Don't you mean *only child*?

Mari: **Oh, yes, I'm sorry.**

Mike: That's OK.

Mari: **I like animals. Have you got *animals?**

Mike: Uhh...no, not right now.

*too shy → a little shy
*a lonely child → an only child
*animals → any animals

麥克: 你一定是王茉莉吧!
茉莉: 是的, 沒錯, 你是?
麥克: 我是麥克・貝爾。我們都在戲劇 101 的班上。
茉莉: 噢! 對, 我想我以前看過你。
麥克: 我都坐在前面。
茉莉: 我很害羞, 所以坐後面。
麥克: 我來自基維斯。
茉莉: 我不知道那個地方。
麥克: 你應該找天去看看, 那裡很漂亮的。
茉莉: 你有沒有兄弟姊妹? 〔你有兄弟和姊妹們對吧? 〕
麥克: 呃……是的, 我確實是有 (兄弟姊妹們)。什麼事?
茉莉: 我是個獨生女。〔我是個寂寞的小孩〕
麥克: 你是說 only child (獨生子女) 嗎?
茉莉: 噢! 是的, 我很抱歉。
麥克: 沒關係的。
茉莉: 我喜歡動物。你有沒有養動物呢?
麥克: 呃……沒有, 現在沒有。

EXAMPLES... EXAMPLES... EXAMPLES...

- Have you got any animals?
  你有養動物嗎?
- Have you got any money?
  你有沒有錢?
- Have you been to any interesting places?
  你有沒有去過什麼好玩的地方?

...NOTES ...NOTES ...NOTES

針對是否有不確定數 (量) 的事物作詢問時, 用 any。

Do you have brothers and sisters? 給人說話者一開始就認定對方既有兄弟也有姊妹, 而且兄 (弟) 姊 (妹) 都各不只一個的感覺。 Have you got animals? 則是泛指所有動物, 意指對方是否養了很多隻 (種) 動物。

Key West: 美國佛羅里達州西南部城市, 作家海明威的故居。

不了，我不喜歡。

No, I don't like it.

Mike: So, you're from Taiwan, Mari.

Mari: **Yes, *in Hualian.**

Mike: Are all the girls as pretty as you over there?

Mari: **Oh, Mike, you are teasing me.**

Mike: No, actually, I really like you.

Mari: **I am *embarrassing.**

Mike: Have some chocolate?

Mari: **No, I don't like.**

Mike: Oh, OK, then let's go for a walk.

Mari: **Yes, yes.**

*in Hualian → from Hualian
*embarrassing → embarrassed

麥克：對了，你是從臺灣來的嘛！茉莉。
茉莉：是啊！從花蓮。
麥克：那邊的女孩子都像你一樣漂亮嗎？
茉莉：噢！麥克，你在取笑我哦！
麥克：不是的，事實上，我真的喜歡你。
茉莉：我會難為情的。
麥克：要不要吃巧克力？
茉莉：不了，我不喜歡。
麥克：噢！好吧！那我們去散散步吧！
茉莉：好啊！好啊！

EXAMPLES... EXAMPLES... EXAMPLES...

- He often comes home late, and I don't like it.
  他經常晚歸，這點我不喜歡。
- The bread is stale —— I can't eat it.
  麵包已經硬掉了 —— 我沒辦法吃了。
- What did you do with the rubbish? —— I threw it away.
  你怎麼處理那（些）個垃圾？ —— 我把它〔他們〕丟掉了。

...NOTES ...NOTES ...NOTES

通常英語中不會省略作受詞的代名詞，但是也有一些普通動詞會將作受詞使用的 it 加以省略，如 I know, I remember, I think, I suppose 等。

I asked a man the way, but he didn't know.
我向一名男子問路，可是他不清楚。

3

我來美國之前住在臺北。

I lived in Taipei before I came to America.

Mike: So what's it like in Hualian?

Mari: **Oh, it is *too beautiful.**

Mike: Too beautiful?

Mari: **Yes, someday please *come to me there.**

Mike: Ah, umm, yeah, sure, I'd like that.

Mari: **But I used to live in Taipei before I came to America.**

Mike: Taipei. I've heard of Taipei.

Mari: **It's a very busy city with lots of people.**

*too beautiful → so/very beautiful
*come to me → visit me

麥克：對了，花蓮是個什麼樣的地方？
茉莉：噢！那裡非常美麗。〔太過美麗了〕
麥克：太過美麗？
茉莉：是啊！哪天到那裡來看我。
麥克：啊！唔，是呀！當然，我很樂意。
茉莉：不過我來美國之前住在臺北。
麥克：臺北。我聽說過臺北。
茉莉：那是個很熱鬧、有很多人的城市。

EXAMPLES... EXAMPLES... EXAMPLES...

- I used to go to school in Leeds when I was a boy.
  當我還是個小男孩時，我上里茲的學校。
- We used to live in London, but now we live in Leeds.
  我們以前住在倫敦，不過現在住在里茲。
- He didn't use to smoke but now he does.
  他以前不抽菸的，不過現在抽了。

...NOTES ...NOTES ...NOTES

used to～的意思是指「過去的習慣、狀態」，因此不可以和表示「確實次數、期間」的字詞連用。也就是說 I used to go to Italy. 一句如果要加上 three times，則動詞就必須改成過去式 I went to Italy three times.

I went to school in Leeds for eight years.

我在里茲的學校待了 8 年。

4

坐飛機只要 40 分鐘。

It's just a forty-minute flight.

Mike: Is Hualian very far from Taipei?

Mari: **No, it's just a forty minutes flight.**

Mike: Don't you mean a *forty-minute flight*?

Mari: **Oh, yes. My teacher always corrected me too.**

Mike: Well, I can't speak a word of Mandarin, so I can't complain.

Mari: **Mike, it's getting cold.**

Mike: Here, you can wear my coat.

Mari: **Oh, you are *kindness to me.**

*kindness to me → so/very kind to me

麥克: 花蓮離臺北很遠嗎?
茉莉: 不會, 坐飛機只要 40 分鐘。
麥克: 你是說 forty-minute flight 嗎?
茉莉: 噢! 是的。我的老師也是不時糾正我。
麥克: 嗯! 我一句中國話也不會講, 所以沒資格說什麼。
茉莉: 麥克, 愈來愈冷了吔!
麥克: 來, 穿上我的外套。
茉莉: 噢! 你對我真好。

EXAMPLES... EXAMPLES... EXAMPLES...

- 時間: a ten-minute walk
  10 分鐘的步行路程
- 距離: a six-mile walk
  6 英里遠的步行
- 年齡: a twenty-year-old man
  20 歲的男人
- 面積・體積: a two-litre car
  2000c.c.的車
- 長度・深度: a twelve-inch ruler
  12 吋長的尺
- 重量: a five-kilo bag of flour
  5 公斤的麵粉袋
- 錢: a five-pound note
  5 英鎊的紙鈔
- 其他: a five-storey building
  5 層樓的建築物

...NOTES ...NOTES ...NOTES

當「數字」和「量詞」(表示計量單位的名詞) 中間以連字號相連時, 就變成了表示時間、尺寸、重量等的「形容詞」。

此時的量詞通常作單數。

5 我媽和我爸結婚了。

My mother married my father.

Mike: Mari, tell me a little about your family.

Mari: **I have a little dog, my mother and my father.**

Mike: How did your parents meet?

Mari: **In Taiwan many people are matched together by their parents or relatives.**

Mike: Wow! That's far out!

Mari: **So my mother married with my father after they were matched together.**

Mike: And do they get along well?

Mari: **I think so, but my mother often says something like, "I *have married you for twenty five years and I still don't know what goes on inside your head."**

*have married you → have been married to you

麥克: 談點關於你家人的事吧！
茉莉: 我家有一隻狗，我媽媽和我爸爸。
麥克: 你爸媽當初怎麼認識的？
茉莉: 在臺灣不少人都是透過雙親或親戚的介紹結婚的。
麥克: 哇！真是無法想像。
茉莉: 所以我媽在相親後就和我爸結婚了。
麥克: 那他們相處得好嗎？
茉莉: 我想是吧！可是我媽常向我爸這麼說:「我嫁給你 25 年了，可是還是不知道你腦子裡在想些什麼。」

EXAMPLES... EXAMPLES... EXAMPLES...

- Will you marry me?
  你願意跟我結婚〔嫁給我，娶我〕嗎？
- Clara didn't marry until she was 40.
  克拉拉直到 40 歲才結婚。
- Meg has been married to John for ten years.
  梅格嫁給約翰 10 年了。
- When are you going to get married?
  你（們）打算何時結婚？

...NOTES ...NOTES ...NOTES

marry「（和……）結婚」（動作）使用時不須加上介系詞。「（和……）結了婚」（狀態）用 be married (to...) 表示。

get married (to...)「（和……）結婚」為通俗的說法，尤其常用於後面沒有受詞銜接時。

6 你該上床了。

It's time you went to bed.

在接待家庭史密斯家裡

Mari: **Can I help with the washing Mrs. Smith?**

Meg: Oh, that's very sweet of you.

Mari: **I like washing the dishes.**

Meg: Don't remind me, or I might get spoiled.

Mari: **I don't understand.**

Meg: Nothing important. Well, how was your day?

Mari: **I made a new friend at the library.**

Meg: Oh, and who would that be?

Mari: **His name is Mike, Mike Bell.**

Meg: Oh, a boy. Is he good looking?

Mari: **Yes, I think so. He helped me with my English.**

Meg: That's very nice of him....(yawns)

Mari: **Mrs. Smith, it's time you go to bed. Let me finish.**

Meg: Oh, Mari, you are an angel.

茉莉: 我來幫你洗好嗎? 史密斯太太?
梅格: 噢! 你真是體貼。
茉莉: 我喜歡洗碗。
梅格: 別提醒我, 我會當真的。
茉莉: 我不懂你的意思。
梅格: 沒什麼! 嗯! 你今天過得怎麼樣?
茉莉: 我在圖書館認識了個朋友。
梅格: 哦! 是個什麼樣的人?
茉莉: 他名字叫做麥克, 麥克·貝爾。
梅格: 哦! 是個男孩子。他長得好看嗎?
茉莉: 是的, 我認為是。他教我英文。
梅格: 他人真好……(打呵欠)
茉莉: 史密斯太太, 你該上床了。剩下的讓我來收拾好了。
梅格: 噢! 茉莉, 你真是個好孩子。

EXAMPLES... EXAMPLES... EXAMPLES...

- Why are you still in bed? It's time you got up.
  你怎麼還窩在床上? 該起來了。
- It's nearly midnight. It's time we went home.
  快要午夜了。我們該回家了。
- It's time I had a holiday.
  我該休個假了。

...NOTES ...NOTES ...NOTES

It is time 後面緊接著主詞 + 動詞時, 用過去式 (假設語氣過去), 內容指的是現在而不是過去。

It's time you went to bed. 「(睡覺的時間已經過了) 你早該上床了」, 改成 It's time to go to bed. 之後, 則意思變成「睡覺的時間到了」, 不管是對說話者還是聽者而言, 都「該上床了」的意思。

7

她說她也許會晚點才到。

She told me that she might be late.

John: Hey pretty lady, you want a ride home?

Mari: **Oh, *Mr. John! You *astonished me!**

John: I saw you sitting here at the bus stop.

Mari: **I'm waiting for my friend, Joanna.**

John: What time did she say she would be here?

Mari: **Around three, but she told that she might be late.**

John: *Told me.*

Mari: **Told you?**

John: Oh, nothing. So are you going to wait for her or do want a ride home?

Mari: **Joanna *said me to wait.**

John: *Told me.*

Mari: **Told you? Are you feeling OK, *Mr. John?**

John: Yes, Mari, I'm fine. OK, I'll see you later.

*Mr. John → John/Mr. Smith
*astonished me → surprised me
*said me → told me
*Mr. John → John/Mr. Smith

約翰: 嘿! 美女, 要不要我載你回家呀?
茉莉: 啊! 約翰先生! 你嚇了我一跳!
約翰: 我看到你坐在公車站牌旁。
茉莉: 我在等我的朋友, 喬安娜。
約翰: 她說她幾點會到?
茉莉: 3 點左右, 但是她說她也許會晚點才到。
約翰: Told me 才對。〔告訴了我〕
茉莉: 告訴了你?
約翰: 噢! 沒事。所以你要等她還是要搭便車回家?
茉莉: 喬安娜叫我等她。
約翰: Told me (叫我) 。〔告訴了我〕
茉莉: 告訴了你? 你還好吧! 約翰先生?
約翰: 是的, 茉莉, 我很好。 OK, 那回頭見囉!

EXAMPLES... EXAMPLES... EXAMPLES...

- He told us that he was getting married.
  他告訴我們他要結婚了。
- You haven't told us what you want.
  你還沒跟我們說你要什麼。
- I've told them where to get off.
  我已經告訴他們在哪裡下車。
- She told the children to stop talking.
  她叫孩子們不要講話。

...NOTES ...NOTES ...NOTES

tell 「告訴～」後面須銜接受詞「所告訴的人」。

say 則是直接加上 that～ (what～等), 表示所傳達的內容。

He said that he was getting married.

他說他就要結婚了。

tell 另外還有「叫……做～」的祈使用法。(語氣比ask, require 更強)

8 我可以打開窗戶嗎？

Would you mind my opening the window?

Mari: **Good morning, Mrs. Smith!**

Meg: Hi, Mari. Did you sleep well?

Mari: **Yes, very well, thank you.**

Meg: By the way, Mari, you don't have to call me Mrs. Smith.

Mari: **Thank you, *Mrs. Meg.**

Meg: Not Mrs. Meg, just Meg.

Mari: **Oh, I see. It's a beautiful day today.**

Meg: Yes, it is.

Mari: **Would you mind opening the window?**

Meg: Mari, you're closer. Why don't you open it yourself?

Mari: **Excuse me....?**

*Mrs. Meg → Meg

茉莉: 早安, 史密斯太太!
梅格: 嗨! 茉莉。你睡得好嗎?
茉莉: 是的, 很好, 謝謝你。
梅格: 對了, 茉莉, 你不需要叫我史密斯太太的。
茉莉: 謝謝你, 梅格太太。
梅格: 不是梅格太太, 梅格就好。
茉莉: 噢! 我懂了。今天天氣真好。
梅格: 是啊! 真的不錯。
茉莉: 我可以打開窗戶嗎? 〔你可不可以開窗呢?〕
梅格: 茉莉, 你比較近, 為什麼不自己打開呢?
茉莉: 咦! 你是說……?

EXAMPLES... EXAMPLES... EXAMPLES...

- Would you mind opening the window?
  (= Please open the window.)
  你可不可以打開窗戶?
- Do you mind my smoking in the kitchen?
  你介意我在廚房抽菸嗎?
  —— No, go ahead.
  —— 不會, 請自便。/不介意。
- Would you mind not smoking?
  (= Please don't smoke.)
  你可不可以不要抽菸?

...NOTES ...NOTES ...NOTES

Would (Do) you mind～ing?「你可不可以～?」意思是指對對方有所請求, 如果是改成 my opening 等指定「由誰來 open」的字詞, 則語意頓時變成「……可以做～嗎」, 成為徵求「許可」的意思。

9 在臺灣都是全體起立的。

Everybody stands up in Taiwan.

John: Is school here different from Taiwan, Mari?
Mari: **Yes, very different.**
John: How so?
Mari: **Well, when the teacher comes in all stand up in Taiwan.**
John: When I was a kid it was the same here.
Mari: **Really? I didn't know that.**
John: At some schools they still do that, though.
Meg: Mari, there's a package for you from Taiwan.
Mari: **Thank you. It's from my mother.**
Meg: Well, open it up.
Mari: **It's all Hualian sweet-potato.**
Meg: Yum. These are good!
Mari: ***I present them to you. All is yours.**
John: Music anyone? What do you like, Mari?
Mari: **I like *every music.**

*I present them to you. All is yours. → Please take them. They're all for you.
*every music → all kinds of music

約翰：這裡的學校和臺灣不一樣嗎？茉莉？
茉莉：是的，非常不一樣。
約翰：怎麼說？
茉莉：嗯！老師進來時，在臺灣都是全體起立的。
約翰：我小的時候這裡也是一樣。
茉莉：真的？我不知道有那種事。
約翰：不過有些學校現在還是如此。
梅格：茉莉，有你的包裹，從臺灣寄來的。
茉莉：謝謝你。是我媽寄來的。
梅格：那麼打開來看看吧！
茉莉：全部都是花蓮薯。
梅格：嗯！這些真好吃。
茉莉：送給你們，這些全部都給你們。
約翰：想聽誰的音樂嗎？你喜歡哪一類的，茉莉？
茉莉：我每一種音樂都喜歡。

EXAMPLES... EXAMPLES... EXAMPLES...

- Everybody enjoyed the party.
  每個人都盡情享受派對。
- Everything is yours.
  都給你。
- He thinks he knows everything.
  他以為他什麼都知道。
- All bread gets stale quickly.
  所有麵包都硬得很快。

...NOTES ...NOTES ...NOTES

all「全員／全體」通常（特別是在口語中）不單獨使用。形容「人」時，可以用 everybody 或是 all the people；形容「物」時則是用 everything。

every 含有「每一個」的意思，因此不可以用在不可數名詞上，此時可以用 all「所有」代替。

10

英文文法比其他語言還要難懂。

English grammar is more difficult to understand than others.

Mike: Mari, can you help me with this math problem?

Mari: **OK, Mike, but only if you help me with my English.**

Mike: OK, it's a deal.

Mari: **I just don't understand this grammar.**

Mike: Let me see.

Mari: **In Taiwan they teach us S+V+O+C things.**

Mike: It sounds like a math problem to me. Here, look, this is the answer.

Mari: **But why? In Mandarin it's the other way around.**

Mike: Well, that's language for you.

Mari: **I think English grammar is more difficult to understand than the others.**

Mike: Which others?

Mari: **Huh?**

麥克：茉莉，你可不可以教我這題數學？
茉莉：可以呀！麥克，如果你教我英文的話。
麥克：OK, 就這麼說定了。
茉莉：我就是弄不懂這個文法。
麥克：讓我瞧瞧。
茉莉：在臺灣，老師教我們的是 S+V+O+C。
麥克：我聽起來像是數學題一樣。好了，這就是答案。
茉莉：為什麼呢？跟中文顛倒吔！
麥克：嗯！語言就是這麼一回事。
茉莉：我想，英文文法比其他語言還要難懂。〔比其他那些語言〕
麥克：哪些語言？
茉莉：咦？

EXAMPLES... EXAMPLES... EXAMPLES...

- Some people enjoy exercise, others don't.
  有人喜歡運動，有人不喜歡。
- You never think of others, only yourself.
  你從沒想到別人，只有你自己。
- Some of the boys were obedient. The others were disobedient.
  那些男孩有些人聽話，剩下的其他人則不守規矩。

...NOTES ...NOTES ...NOTES

others 意思是指「不特定的其他人・物」，但是在加了 the 之後就變成了「特定」。

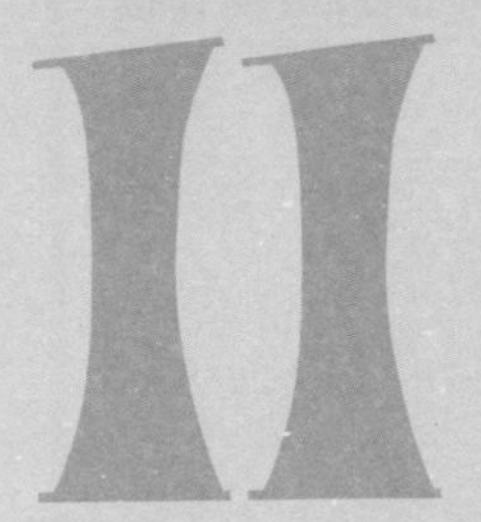

她有著一頭紅髮。

She has red hair.

Mari: **Mike, *thanks for helping me too much.**

Mike: Too much, was it? Then let's go get a coffee.

Mari: **Ann is *too pretty. She has red hairs. Is she *your lover?**

Mike: No! Of course not! We're just friends.

Mari: **Good! She asked me for *an advice.**

Mike: What was that?

Mari: **She likes Richard and asked me *what did I think.**

Mike: Well, good for them. The sky is getting dark again.

Mari: **Yes, we're having *a terrible weather.**

兩人走入一間咖啡廳，侍者詢問他們要點什麼……

Mari: **Could we have *two coffee, please?**

Mike: *Coffees*, Mari, *coffees*.

*thanks for helping me too much → thank you so much for helping me
*too pretty → so pretty *your lover → your girlfriend
*an advice → some advice *what did I think → what I thought
*a terrible weather → terrible weather *two coffee → two coffee

茉莉: 麥克，非常感謝你的幫忙。〔但是幫太多了〕
麥克: 太多，是嗎？那麼我們去喝咖啡好了。
茉莉: 安真是漂亮，有著一頭紅髮，她是你的女朋友嗎？〔情人〕
麥克: 不！當然不是！我們只是普通朋友。
茉莉: 太好了！她要我給她個建議。
麥克: 什麼事？
茉莉: 她喜歡理查，問我覺得如何？
麥克: 嗯！祝福他們囉！天色又要暗下來了。
茉莉: 是啊！快要變天了。

× × ×

茉莉: 請給我們兩杯咖啡。
麥克: Coffees，茉莉，是 coffees。

EXAMPLES... EXAMPLES... EXAMPLES...

- I must wash my hair.
  我該洗頭了。
- She brushed the cat's hairs off her coat.
  她刷掉外套上的貓毛。
- We're going to have stormy weather.
  暴風雨要來了。
- Two teas, please.
  請給我兩杯茶。

...NOTES ...NOTES ...NOTES

advice, weather 等的「不可數名詞」不可以作複數、也不可以加冠詞 a。

hair 「頭髮」當指的是一根一根的毛髮時，作「可數名詞」使用；指的如果是全體頭髮時，則作「不可數名詞」。

coffee, tea 在作餐飲點購時，用作可數名詞。

lover 在口語中多半不用來形容男女朋友的關係，因為該字會讓人產生性伴侶的聯想，尤其當指一名男性為自己的 lover 時，別人可能會誤以為指的是「情夫」。（「情婦」為 mistress）

12

書很貴吔！

Books are very expensive.

Mari: **How can I improve my English, Mike?**

Mike: First I think you need some new books.

Mari: **Why? I have this dictionary from Taiwan.**

Mike: Yes, I know, but it looks a little old.

Mari: **But the books are very expensive.**

Mike: Which books?

Mari: ***All over the world books!**

Mike: Uhh...I don't think I understand.

Mari: **Maybe I should jump *from bridge, Mike.**

Mike: Hey, hold on! Don't scare me.

Mari: **I am joking, ha, ha, ha!**

*All over the world books! → Books everywhere./Books all over the world.

*from bridge → from the bridge

茉莉：我要怎樣才能加強我的英文呢，麥克？
麥克：首先我想你需要一些新書。
茉莉：為什麼？我有這本從臺灣帶來的字典呀！
麥克：是的，我知道，可是它看起來有點舊。
茉莉：可是書很貴吔！〔那些書很……〕
麥克：哪些書？
茉莉：全世界任何地方的書啊！〔世界中的書〕
麥克：呃……我想我聽不懂。
茉莉：也許我該從橋上跳下算了，麥克。
麥克：喂，慢著！別嚇我。
茉莉：我是在開玩笑的，哈，哈，哈！

EXAMPLES... EXAMPLES... EXAMPLES...

- I like cats.
  我喜歡貓。
- Children enjoy games.
  孩子們喜歡遊戲。

...NOTES ...NOTES ...NOTES

取單字所代表的整體意象，而不單獨挑出其中的「哪個」另作說明時，不須加 the。

Cobras are dangerous.

眼鏡蛇是危險的。

the 的用法是使事物特定、具體化。當雙方對話題中所指的事物是哪一個都有共識時，必須加 the。

The snake is dangerous.

那條蛇是危險的。

另外，也可以用「 the ＋ 單數可數名詞」來表示「(那種叫做)～類的事物」作說明。

The cobra is dangerous.

眼鏡蛇是危險的。〔那種叫做眼鏡蛇的蛇類是～〕

13

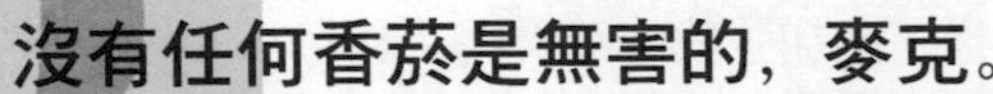

沒有任何香菸是無害的，麥克。

No cigarette is harmless, Mike.

Mari: **Mike, I don't think you should smoke so much.**

Mike: But these cigarettes are harmless. Look, almost no tar or nicotine.

Mari: **I don't know about that, but...**

Mike: I think it is just stress. I'll give it up one of these days.

Mari: **I don't want you to *die quickly, Mike.**

Mike: Ah...I think you mean *soon*, don't you?

Mari: **Anyway, any cigarette is not harmless, Mike.**

Mike: OK, Mari. I'll keep that in mind.

*die quickly → die soon

茉莉：麥克，我想你不該抽那麼多菸的。
麥克：可是這些香菸是無害的。你看，幾乎不含焦油或尼古丁。
茉莉：那種事我是不清楚啦！不過……
麥克：我想是因為壓力吧！我過幾天就戒掉。
茉莉：我不要你早死，麥克。〔迅速地死〕
麥克：呃……我想你是指soon（快〔早〕地），對吧？
茉莉：總而言之，沒有任何香菸是無害的，麥克。
麥克：知道了，茉莉。我會記在心上的。

EXAMPLES... EXAMPLES... EXAMPLES...

- No stamp is required.
  不用貼郵票。
- No system of government is perfect.
  沒有一種政府體制是完美的。
- No one understands me.
  沒有人了解我。
- Nobody phoned, did they?
  沒有人打電話給我嗎？

...NOTES ...NOTES ...NOTES

any 不能作「否定句的主詞」使用， no 可以。

（no 的意思和 not any, not a 相當，只是 no 的否定語氣較強）

anybody/nobody, anything/nothing 等也是相同的用法。

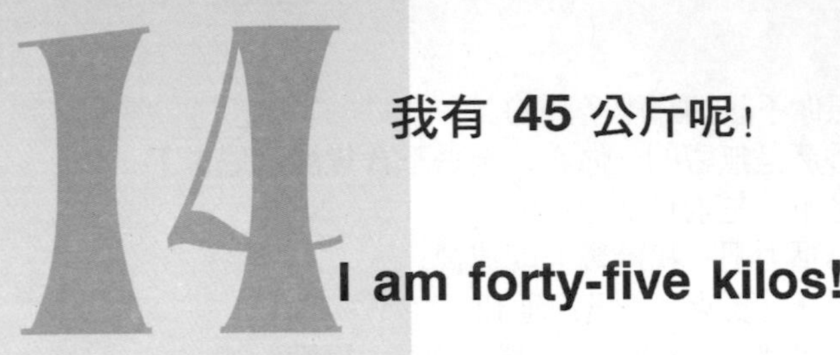

14 我有 45 公斤呢！

I am forty-five kilos!

Mari: ***How high are you Mike?**

Mike: Me? I'm ahh, 5 foot eight. Why?

Mari: **You are so *big!**

Mike: Not really. Most of my friends are taller.

Mari: **I'm so *small.**

Mike: You're just right for me, Mari.

Mari: **Do you think so?**

Mike: Yes, I do. How much do you weigh anyway?

Mari: **I'm too fat! I have forty-five kilos!**

Mike: Ah...how much is that in pounds?

Mari: ***I don't understand pounds.**

Mike: Well, it's not that important. Let's go get some cheesecake and put on some weight.

Mari: **Oh, Mike. You eat too much!**

*How high → How tall
*big → tall
*small → short
*I don't understand pounds. → I'm not familiar with pounds.

茉莉：你有多高啊？麥克？
麥克：我？我有呃，5 呎 8。怎樣？
茉莉：你好高大唷！〔好大唷〕
麥克：沒有的事。我多數的朋友都比我高。
茉莉：我就很矮。〔很小〕
麥克：你對我來說剛剛好，茉莉。
茉莉：你這麼認為？
麥克：是啊！對了，你有多重？
茉莉：我太胖了！我有 45 公斤呢！
麥克：呃……那是幾磅？
茉莉：我不清楚英磅怎麼算吔！
麥克：算了，那不重要。我們去吃點起司蛋糕增加體重吧！
茉莉：噢！麥克。你吃太多了。

EXAMPLES... EXAMPLES... EXAMPLES...

- How much do you weigh?
  你多重？
- —— I am sixty-five kilos (in weight)./ I weigh 65 kilos.
  我有 65 公斤（重）。／我重 65 公斤。
- —— I weighed 100 pounds two months ago.
  2 個月前我的體重是 100 磅。
- How tall is your son?
  你兒子有多高？
- —— He's five feet seven (inches tall).
  他有 5 呎 7（吋高）。

...NOTES ...NOTES ...NOTES

形容身高、體重時，通常主詞是人，動詞用 be 動詞。
除了 How 之外，另外也可以用what 來提問。
What is your height [weight]?
你身高〔體重〕多少？
（ How much is your height? 是錯誤的用法）

15

他過來了！

Here he comes!

Peg: Hey, Mari! Why are you all alone?

Mari: **Hello, Peg, I'm just waiting for the bus.**

Peg: Well, let's go back together. Number 42, right?

Mari: **Yes, 42. But why are you taking the bus?**

Peg: I broke up with Chris, so now it's back to riding the bus.

Mari: **Chris! Oh, here** comes he!

Peg: Don't look, Mari. Just ignore him.

Mari: **Oh, OK.**

Peg: Who needs boys?!

Mari: **Look, Peg! *Here our bus comes!**

Peg: Lucky us. Quick! Let's go.

*Here our bus comes! → Here comes our bus!

佩格: 嗨! 茱莉! 你怎麼一個人?
茱莉: 哈囉, 佩格, 我正在等公車。
佩格: 那我們一起回去吧! 42 號公車對嗎?
茱莉: 是呀! 42。不過你為什麼要搭公車呢?
佩格: 我跟克利斯吹了, 所以就又回來搭公車了啊!
茱莉: 克利斯! 噢! 他過來了。
佩格: 別看, 茱莉, 不要理他。
茱莉: 噢! OK。
佩格: 誰需要男生!
茱莉: 看, 佩格! 我們的公車來了!
佩格: 我們真幸運。快點! 走吧!

EXAMPLES... EXAMPLES... EXAMPLES...

- Here it comes.
  來了。
- Here we are.
  我們到了。
- Here it is.
  請用。/在這裡。
- Here comes Mr. Jones.
  瓊斯先生來了。
- Oh good — here comes the bus.
  太好了 — 公車來了。
- There goes your brother.
  你哥〔弟〕走過去了。

...NOTES ...NOTES ...NOTES

以 Here, There 等起始的句子, 主詞如果是名詞, 則動詞置於主詞前; 主詞如果是代名詞, 則動詞接在主詞之後。

16

所有人都回家了。

Everybody has gone home already.

Meg: Mari, what are you doing here?

Mari: **I'm washing the dishes, Meg.**

Meg: Oh, I'll take care of this. You go back to your friends.

Mari: **Everybody** have gone **home already.**

Meg: Everybody has, Mari. Everybody has.

Mari: **Oh, I'm sorry.**

Meg: Don't be sorry. Just remember.

Mari: **OK, I'll try.**

Meg: Did you have a good time?

Mari: **Yes, thank you very much for letting them come here.**

Meg: Anytime you want, Mari.

梅格：茉莉，你在這裡做什麼？
茉莉：我在洗碗，梅格。
梅格：噢！這些我來做就好了。你回去你朋友那裡。
茉莉：所有人都回家了。
梅格：Everybody has，茉莉。 Everybody has。
茉莉：噢！我很抱歉。
梅格：用不著抱歉。記住就好。
茉莉：OK，我會努力的。
梅格：你今天玩得開心嗎？
茉莉：是的，非常感謝你讓他們來這裡。
梅格：只要你高興隨時都可以，茉莉。

EXAMPLES... EXAMPLES... EXAMPLES...

- Everybody in this street has a car.
  這條街上的每個人都有部車。
- Everybody has made up their minds [his or her mind].
  每個人都下定決心了。
- Has everyone got their tickets?
  每個人都拿到車票了嗎？

...NOTES ...NOTES ...NOTES

Everybody, everyone 「所有的人，每個人」一般作單數，「動詞」也用單數。

但是由於語意給人的感覺是複數，口語中承接的「代名詞」常改成複數。

17

我得剪個頭髮。

I must get my hair cut.

Mari: **Mrs. Smith, Mike asked me out to dinner with him.**

Meg: Oh, that's nice. Where is he taking you?

Mari: **He said he knows a nice Italian place by the lake.**

Meg: Well don't stay out too late.

Mari: **But Mrs. Smith, I must** cut my hair, **and I don't know where.**

Meg: You know it's not that expensive to have it done at the hairdresser's.

Mari: **I'm sorry, I don't understand.**

Meg: I mean that you don't have to cut it yourself.

Mari: **Cut it myself?!**

茉莉：史密斯太太，麥克約我出去吃晚餐。
梅格：哦！很好嘛。他打算帶你去哪裡？
茉莉：他說他知道湖邊有家不錯的義大利餐館。
梅格：嗯！別玩得太晚。
茉莉：可是史密斯太太，我得剪個頭髮；還有，我不知道去哪裡剪才好。
梅格：你知道上美容院給人家剪髮不貴的。
茉莉：對不起，我不明白。
梅格：我是說你不用自己動手剪。
茉莉：我自己剪？！

EXAMPLES... EXAMPLES... EXAMPLES...

- Go and get your hair cut! (= Go and get a haircut!)
  你該去理頭了。
- I must get my shirt mended.
  我該找人補補我的襯衫了。
- I'm having my tooth taken out tomorrow.
  我明天要去拔牙。
- Sue had her eyes tested yesterday.
  蘇昨天檢查了眼睛。

...NOTES ...NOTES ...NOTES

「get/have ＋ O ＋ 過去分詞」意思是「由別人為自己做～」。get/have 發成重音。（陳述過去事實時通常用 had）

下面例句是類似的用法。

I would like this letter typed before tomorrow.

明天之前把這封信打好。

18 那件綠色洋裝多少錢？

What's the price of the green dress?

Clerk: Hello, may I help you?

Mari: **Well, I'm looking for a nice dress.**

Clerk: A special occasion?

Mari: **I'm going on my first date in America.**

Clerk: Oh, well, that is special.

Mari: **What's the cost of that green dress?**

Clerk: I can't tell you the cost, but I can tell you the price.

Mari: **I'm sorry. I don't understand.**

Clerk: Oh, nothing serious. It's 54 dollars.

Mari: **Can you raise the hem for me?**

Clerk: Of course. We can do it while you wait.

Mari: **OK. *I'm hot, so I'll sit in the *shadow of that tree outside.**

Clerk: You wait anywhere you want. But let me measure you first.

*I'm hot → It's hot
*shadow → shade

店員: 您好，我能為您服務嗎?
茉莉: 嗯! 我想找一件好看的洋裝。
店員: 特殊場合要穿的?
茉莉: 我要去赴我來美國後的第一次約會。
店員: 噢! 那的確特殊。
茉莉: 那件綠色洋裝多少錢? 〔成本多少? 〕
店員: 我不能告訴您成本，不過我可以告訴您它的售價。
茉莉: 對不起，我不懂您的意思。
店員: 噢! 沒什麼。售價是54 美元。
茉莉: 您可以幫我把裙襬改短嗎?
店員: 當然可以，如果您願意等的話。
茉莉: OK。好熱喔! 我到外面的樹下乘涼坐一下。
店員: 看您想在哪裡等都行。不過先讓我量一下尺寸。

EXAMPLES... EXAMPLES... EXAMPLES...

- What is the price of this camera?
  這臺相機價格多少?
- The cost of running a car goes up every year.
  養一部車的成本年年增高。
- What is the charge for a telephone call?
  打一通電話要多少錢?
- What's the fare from Taipei to Tokyo?
  從臺北到東京的運費是多少?

...NOTES ...NOTES ...NOTES

cost 的意思是「做～所需的總金額」。(成本，費用，開銷)
price 意思是「針對某物所需的支付」。(價格)
charge 指的是「被索求的東西」。(服務費)
「交通費」是 fare; 「入場費、學費、看診費」是 fee。
另外，日蔭是 shade; shadow 指的是「輪廓清晰的」影子，「黑影」。

19

我總是帶把傘以防會下雨。

I always take an umbrella in case it rains.

John: Good morning, Mari.

Mari: **Good morning, Mr. uh, ah, John.**

John: I heard you're seeing Mike tonight.

Mari: **I think *I'm loving him.**

John: Uh, I see, well, don't be too hasty, now.

Mari: **I don't understand.**

John: Oh, nothing really. Meg will explain later.

Mari: **OK. Anyway, I have to go now.**

John: Mari, it's a beautiful day today. Do you really need that umbrella?

Mari: **I always take an umbrella in case it will rain.**

John: Oh, I see. Oh, well. Have a nice day.

Mari: **I will!**

*I'm loving him → I'm in love with him

約翰：早安，茉莉。
茉莉：早安，呃！啊！約翰先生。
約翰：我聽說你今晚要和麥克約會。
茉莉：我想我愛上他了。
約翰：呃！是這樣子的呀！嗯！現在不要太心急。
茉莉：我不懂。
約翰：噢！沒什麼的。梅格以後會跟你解釋的。
茉莉：OK。總之我現在必須走了。
約翰：茉莉，今天天氣好極了。你真的需要那把傘嗎？
茉莉：我總是帶把傘以防會下雨。
約翰：噢！我懂了。噢！嗯！祝你有個愉快的一天。
茉莉：我會的。

EXAMPLES... EXAMPLES... EXAMPLES...

- I'll draw a map for you in case you can't find our house.
  我會畫張地圖給你，以免你找不到我們家。
- I don't want to go out tonight in case Mike phones.
  我今晚不出去了，以防麥克可能打電話來。

...NOTES ...NOTES ...NOTES

in case 用在表示「預先做～以防可能發生的事」，後面接續的雖然是未來發生的事，動詞仍須用「現在式」，不可以用 will。

美式英語中，in case 有時也等於 if「倘若，萬一」。

In case Mike phones, tell him I'm out.

萬一麥克打電話來，就告訴他我出去了。

20

我現在要走了，免得遲到。

I'm going to leave now, so as not to be late.

Peg: Well, Mari, how do you feel before your first date in America?

Mari: **Oh, Peg, I'm *too nervous.**

Peg: Don't be silly, just remember everything I told you.

Mari: **I'll try. I wrote it all in my notebook.**

Peg: Don't let him kiss you on the first date, OK?

Mari: **Ah, OK, I think.**

Peg: And he pays for everything, right.

Mari: **He pays. OK.**

Peg: And don't stay out too late.

Mari: **Peg, you *are sounding like my mother!**

Peg: Someday you'll thank me.

Mari: **Well, I'm going to leave now, not to be late.**

Peg: Good luck!

*too nervous → very nervous
*are sounding like → sound like

佩格：嗯！茱莉，就要去赴在美國的第一次約會了，心情如何？
茱莉：噢！佩格，我好緊張。
佩格：別傻了，只要記得所有我告訴過你的話。
茱莉：我試試看。那些話我全都記在筆記本上了。
佩格：別讓他在第一次約會就親你， OK？
茱莉：啊——， OK，我想 OK。
佩格：還有錢全部由他付，知道嗎？
茱莉：由他付。 OK。
佩格：而且別玩得太晚。
茱莉：佩格，你好像我媽哦！
佩格：有天你會感謝我的。
茱莉：好了，我現在要走了，免得遲到。
佩格：祝你幸運！

EXAMPLES... EXAMPLES... EXAMPLES...

- She ran down the street so as not to miss the bus.
  她在街上用跑的，免得錯過公車了。
- I left early in order not to be late for class。
  我早早出門，免得上課遲到。
- He just kept quiet in order not to upset her.
  為了不想讓她失望，他只是保持沈默。

...NOTES ...NOTES ...NOTES

表示「為了得以～」的 to～用法，其否定形「為了不致〔免得〕～」不可以直接加 not 改成 not to～，通常都是用 so as not to～ /in order not to～。

not to～作否定目的使用的情形不多，僅見於接續 careful 後面等幾個固定的用法。

Be careful not to break the eggs.

小心別打破蛋。

21

謝謝你帶我來這裡。

Thanks for bringing me here!

第一次的約會

Mari: **Wow, Mike, this is such a beautiful place!**

Mike: I'm glad you like it, Mari. The city is so noisy.

Mari: **And there are so many people.**

Mike: We just don't have much time to talk to each other.

Mari: **That's right. We've never been alone before.**

Mike: I hope you don't mind, but I'm actually very fond of you.

Mari: **Oh, Mike, thanks for taking me here!**

Mike: What?! Just a minute, Mari, I, ahh...

Mari: **What's the matter, Mike?**

茉莉: 哇！麥克，這真是個漂亮的地方！
麥克: 我很高興你喜歡，城市裡頭太吵了。
茉莉: 而且人又好多。
麥克: 我們兩人連好好說話的時間都沒有。
茉莉: 真的吔！我們以前從來沒有單獨一起過。
麥克: 希望你不要介意，可是我真的非常喜歡你。
茉莉: 噢！麥克，謝謝你帶我來這裡！〔要在這裡佔有我〕
麥克: 什麼?! 慢著，茉莉，我，呃……
茉莉: 你怎麼啦，麥克？

EXAMPLES... EXAMPLES... EXAMPLES...

- Let's have another drink, and I'll take you home.
  我們再喝一杯，然後我就送你回家。
- Can you bring the car to my house tomorrow?
  你明天可以把車帶來我家嗎？
- Barbara, would you come here, please?
  芭芭拉，請你過來這裡好嗎？
  —— I'm coming.
  —— 我來了。

...NOTES ...NOTES ...NOTES

bring 是朝著說話者／聽者所在處趨近的意思； take 指的是朝其他方向移動的動作。 come/go 的用法則和 bring 相同。

在電話交談中，動作的方向性以對方的角度出發。

A: Don't worry, George. Come and join us. Oh, yes, don't forget to bring something to drink, right?
別擔心了，喬治。來加入我們嘛！噢！對了，別忘了帶點喝的東西來，知道嗎？

B: Right. I'm coming around 8, and I'll bring a bottle of wine. Is that all right?
知道了。我 8 點鐘左右過去，而且我會帶一瓶酒。這樣可以嗎？

22

很高興見到您，教授。

Nice seeing you, Professor.

Prof: So, Mari, how are you settling in to life here in America?

Mari: **Oh, Professor, I'm *enjoying so much.**

Prof: Well, I'm glad to hear that.

Mari: **Everyone is so kind and helpful.**

Prof: Are you keeping up with the courses?

Mari: **Some things are still difficult to understand, but....**

Prof: Oh, I'm sure you'll get used to it.

Mari: **Yes, you're right, Professor.**

Prof: Well, I must be off. Nice talking to you.

Mari: **It is nice to see you, Professor. Bye.**

*enjoying → enjoying myself

教授：對了，茉莉，在美國的生活還習慣嗎？
茉莉：噢！教授，我非常樂在其中。
教授：嗯！我很高興聽你這麼說。
茉莉：每個人都好親切，而且都很幫忙。
教授：課業跟得上嗎？
茉莉：還是有些難懂的地方，不過……
教授：噢！我相信你會習慣的。
茉莉：是的，正如您所說的，教授。
教授：嗯！我該走了。很高興和你聊天。
茉莉：很高興見到您，教授。 Bye。

EXAMPLES... EXAMPLES... EXAMPLES...

- Nice talking with you, John. Good night.
  很高興和你談話，約翰。晚安。
- Nice to meet you.
  很高興認識您。
- How do you do? —— How do you do?
  您好。——您好。（雙方第一次見面時）
- How nice to see you!
  真高興看到你！（對到訪的客人打招呼）

...NOTES ...NOTES ...NOTES

(It's been) Nice meeting [seeing] you. 「很高興見到您」是分手時的問候語，通常用於初次見面時。

(It is) Nice to meet [see] you. 「很高興認識您」是雙方第一次見面時開口說的第一句話。

但是如果將 is 改成 was，寫成 It was nice to see you. 這時就會變成分手問候語「很高興見到您」的意思。

23 你看來氣呼呼的。

You look angry.

Mari: **Hello, Mike, what's wrong? You look** angrily.

Mike: Oh, hi, Mari. Oh, it's just Professor Jones.

Mari: **I think I understand. He *looked like angry in class.**

Mike: Yes, well, he didn't like the report I wrote.

Mari: **What will happen to you?**

Mike: I have to do it all over again.

Mari: **I'm sorry.**

Mike: Hey, it's not your fault, but I don't think I can see you after school today.

Mari: **That's OK. I should study also.**

Mike: Yes, maybe you should look up *look* and *look like* and *angry* and *angrily.*

*looked like angry → looked angry

茉莉: 哈囉，麥克，怎麼了？你看來氣呼呼的。
麥克: 哦！嗨！茉莉。噢！還不就是瓊斯教授嘛！
茉莉: 我想我能理解，他在課堂上一副生氣的樣子。
麥克: 是啊！唉！他對我的報告不滿意。
茉莉: 那你會怎樣？
麥克: 我必須全部重做。
茉莉: 我很抱歉。
麥克: 喂！又不是你的錯，不過我想我們今天放學後不能見面了。
茉莉: 沒關係。我也應該唸書了。
麥克: 是啊！也許你該查查 look 和look like, angry 和 angrily 的意思。

EXAMPLES... EXAMPLES... EXAMPLES...

- You look very tired —— what's the matter?
  你看起來好累 —— 怎麼了？
- The car looks all right, but it doesn't work.
  車子看來一切正常，可是就是發不動。
- She doesn't want to look stupid.
  她不想（自己）看來一副呆樣。
- She looks just like her mother.
  她簡直就像她母親的翻版。

...NOTES ...NOTES ...NOTES

表示「（樣子、外觀）看起來～」時，用 look，然後後面接形容詞。比方說 look happy 就是「看起來幸福」、look pleased「看起來高興」等。

如果後面接續的不是形容詞而是名詞時，則換成用「look like ＋ 名詞」的形式。

24

我今天早上可以看到她了。

I was able to see her this morning.

Mari: **Hi, *Mrs. Meg.**

Meg: Stop calling me that. Meg is fine.

Mari: **Yes, Meg. I'll try.**

Meg: Any news about the cat you found Friday?

Mari: **I could see her this morning. The doctor said she'll be OK.**

Meg: Good, let's hope someone adopts her. Hand me some eggs, Mari.

Mari: **Actually I could get only six eggs because of the union strike.**

Meg: Listen, before dinner why don't you look up *can* and *be able to.*

Mari: ***Did I mistake again?**

Meg: Uhh.. and *mistake.*

*Mrs. Meg → Meg
*Did I mistake → Did I make a mistake

茉莉：嗨！梅格太太。
梅格：別再那麼叫我，叫我梅格就好。
茉莉：知道了，梅格。我會儘量。
梅格：你在星期五發現的那隻貓後來怎麼了？
茉莉：我今天早上可以看到她了。醫生說她會沒事的。
梅格：太好了，希望有人願意領養她。拿一些蛋給我，茉莉。
茉莉：事實上因為工會罷工的關係，我只能買到 6 個蛋。
梅格：聽著，在吃晚餐前，你要不要去查一查can 和 be able to？
茉莉：我又弄錯了嗎？
梅格：呃……還有 mistake。

EXAMPLES... EXAMPLES... EXAMPLES...

- I was able to borrow an umbrella, so I didn't get wet.
  我借到了一把傘，所以才沒有淋濕。
- The doctor was able to cure her illness.
  那位醫生終於治好了她的病。
- He succeeded in persuading her to do it.
  他成功說服了她去做那件事。

...NOTES ...NOTES ...NOTES

指「（可以／得以）做到～」的單次偶發行為時，不可以用表示「具有做～能力」的 could。

正確用法是配合句子前後文，寫成 was able to 或 succeed 等，有時甚至直接用動詞的過去式也可完整表達出句意。

但是如果是在否定句中，或是與感官動詞 see「看（得）見」，hear「聽（得）見」等連用時，即使所表示的是單次偶發行為，此時一樣可以用 could。

He read the note but couldn't understand it.
他讀了便條，但是不懂得意思。

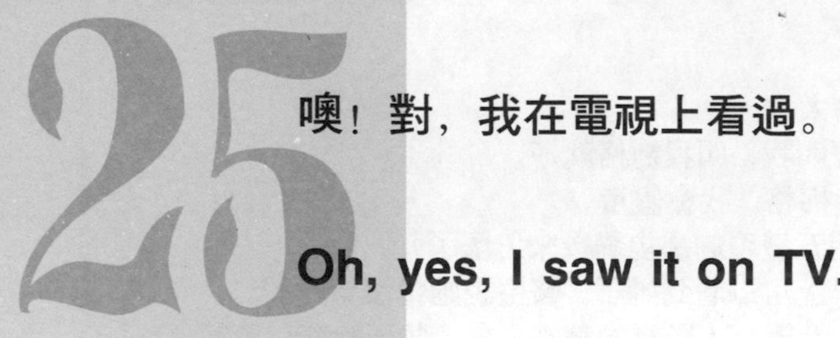

25 噢！對，我在電視上看過。

Oh, yes, I saw it on TV.

Mari: **Hi, Mr. Smith. Anything special in the news?**

John: Well, mostly the same old stuff, but there was one interesting article.

Mari: **What about?**

John: Some old lady who left almost a billion dollars in her inheritance to her cat.

Mari: **Oh, yes, I watched it on TV.**

John: You should say *saw* it on TV. What are you doing anyway?

Mari: **I'm *waiting a call from Mary.**

John: I think you mean *expecting* a call, not *waiting.*

Mari: **Oh, my English is so bad!**

John: Don't get upset. You have to make mistakes to improve.

*waiting a call → waiting for a call

茉莉：嗨！史密斯先生。有沒有什麼特別的新聞？
約翰：嗯！大多都是老樣子，不過有一則有趣的報導。
茉莉：關於什麼的？
約翰：有個老婦人留了近 10 億美金的遺產給她的貓。
茉莉：噢！對，我在電視上看過。
約翰：你應該說在電視上 saw。對了，你在做什麼？
茉莉：我正在等瑪麗的電話。
約翰：我想你是要說 expecting 電話，不是 waiting。
茉莉：噢！我的英文真是糟透了！
約翰：別沮喪。你要出錯才能進步嘛！

EXAMPLES... EXAMPLES... EXAMPLES...

- Did you watch TV last night?
  你昨晚看電視了沒？
- Would you like to watch “News Station”?
  你要不要看 “News Station”？
- I’m expecting a phone call from Mary.
  我正在等瑪麗的電話。

...NOTES ...NOTES ...NOTES

watch 用於表示「持續一段時間注視（動態的物體）」，看電視便是用 watch。

如果受詞換成電視節目時，則 watch，see，enjoy 都可使用。

I saw [watched] the ball game on TV.

我看電視轉播的棒球比賽。

不過下列情況便只能用 see。

I saw your father on TV yesterday.

我昨天在電視上看到你爸爸。

至於 wait/expect 的用法是？下面的例句可以作為參考。

I’m waiting for a phone call.

我正在等一通電話。

26

10 英里走起來很遠吔！

Ten miles is a long way to walk.

Meg: What are you reading, Mari?

Mari: **A book about this area.**

Meg: You should look up Devil's Peak.

Mari: **Is it a nice place?**

Meg: Very beautiful, and near. Just ten miles.

Mari: **Ten miles are a long way to walk.**

Meg: Are you kidding? How old are you anyway?

Mari: **I will ask Mike to take me.**

Meg: Do that. But there's some bad news on TV.

Mari: **Yes, I heard. More than one person *are going to lose his job at the factory.**

Meg: Yeah, the economy is just getting worse.

Mari: **I'm sure it will get better.**

Meg: I'm glad you think so.

*are → is

梅格：你在看什麼，茱莉？
茱莉：一本介紹這地區的書。
梅格：那你應該查查 Devil's Peak。
茱莉：那是個好地方嗎？
梅格：非常漂亮，而且又近。才 10 英里而已。
茱莉：10 英里走起來很遠吔！
梅格：你在開玩笑吧！你都幾歲了？
茱莉：我會找麥克帶我去的。
梅格：就那麼辦。不過電視上有些壞消息。
茱莉：是啊！我聽說了。工廠有好多人即將失業。
梅格：是啊！經濟情況愈來愈糟糕。
茱莉：我相信會好轉的。
梅格：如果真那樣就好了。

EXAMPLES... EXAMPLES... EXAMPLES...

- Three years is too long to wait.
  要等 3 年太漫長了。
- Two hundred pounds is a lot to spend on a dress.
  一件衣服花費 200 鎊太多了。
- 90 miles an hour is much too fast.
  時速90 英里太快了。

...NOTES ...NOTES ...NOTES

不管是距離、期間、金錢、速度還是重量等，只要是被視為「一個整體的數量」時，即使名詞的形式為複數，仍然視同「一個單位」，作單數使用。也就是說動詞、代名詞等都必須用單數。

more than one～也是作單數使用。

More than one person was injured.

不只一個人受了傷。

27 小孩子都不免調皮的呀！

All children can be naughty.

Mari: **Mr. Smith, why don't you have children?**

John: Ah, Mari, that's a difficult question.

Mari: **Don't you like children?**

John: Of course we do, though they can be a little naughty sometimes.

Mari: All of children **can be naughty.**

John: Umm, yes, that may be true, but...

Mari: **I love *the children.**

John: Which children?

Mari: **Huh?**

*the children → children

茱莉: 史密斯先生，你們為什麼不生小孩呢?
約翰: 噢! 茱莉，那是個很難回答的問題。
茱莉: 你們不喜歡小孩子嗎?
約翰: 當然喜歡，雖然他們有時蠻調皮的。
茱莉: 小孩子都不免調皮的呀!
約翰: 嗯! 是啊! 也許真是如此，不過……
茱莉: 我喜歡小孩。〔我喜歡那些小孩〕
約翰: 哪些小孩?
茱莉: 咦?

EXAMPLES... EXAMPLES... EXAMPLES...

- All children love ice-cream.
  所有小孩都喜歡冰淇淋。
- All passengers are requested to remain seated.
  所有乘客都被要求坐在位子上。
- All (of) my friends live in London.
  我的朋友全部住在倫敦。
- She drank all (of) the milk.
  她把那些牛奶喝光了。

...NOTES ...NOTES ...NOTES

all「全部的～」後面接續的名詞如果是不受到 the, this, these, my, Tom's 等限定的「一般性事物」，則可以直接用「all + 名詞」的形式。

但是如果是受到限定的「特定事物」，這時就要改成「all + (of) + the 等 + 名詞」的形式。

28 你覺得史匹柏最新的片子如何?

What do you think of Spielberg's latest film?

在茱莉的朋友,佩特家的浴室裡

Mari: **What do you think of Spielberg's last film, Pat?**

Pat: Was it really his last film? I haven't seen it yet.

Mari: **I liked it very much.**

Pat: What was it about?

Mari: **About a girl who likes *elder men, and....**

Pat: *Older* men, Mari.

Mari: **Yes, and she spends years taking care of her *ill mother, and....**

Pat: *Sick* mother.

Mari: **And then one day she decides to climb the *tallest mountain in Europe, and....**

Pat: *Highest* mountain, Mari.

Mari: **By the way, Pat, this is a very *female bathroom!**

Pat: Yeah, that's what my dad says all the time!

*elder → older
*ill → sick
*tallest → highest
*female bathroom → feminine bathroom

茉莉：你覺得史匹柏最新的片子如何？佩特？〔最後的片子……〕
佩特：那部真的是他最後的片子嗎？我還沒看呢！
茉莉：我很喜歡這部電影。
佩特：它內容在講什麼？
茉莉：關於一個喜歡上年長男性的女孩，然後……
佩特：Older men 才對，茉莉。
茉莉：對，然後她長年照顧她生病的母親，然後……
佩特：是sick mother。
茉莉：然後有一天她決定攀登歐洲最高的山，然後……
佩特：Highest mountain，茉莉。
茉莉：對了，佩特，這是間非常女性化的浴室！
佩特：是啊！我爸老是這麼說！

EXAMPLES... EXAMPLES... EXAMPLES...

- What's the latest news of Charles?
  查爾斯的近況如何？
- Who's the elder of the two children?
  這兩個小孩中哪個年紀較大？
- He is now a very sick man.
  他現在病得非常嚴重。
- She is so feminine.
  她非常的女性化。

...NOTES ...NOTES ...NOTES

latest 意思是「最新的」； last 是「最後的」。

elder 「年長的」用於家族成員之間的輩份關係。

ill 不可直接用於名詞前， sick 則可以。

形容人的身高、樹木等的高度「高」時，用 tall；有時形容建築物細高時也用 tall。 high 指的是高於地面的東西，不可用於人的身上。

female 表示性別「女性的」； feminine 則是指舉止、氣質等「女性化的」。

29

她很抱歉無法和你碰面。

She was sorry to have missed you.

Mari: **Hi, Mike. What are you doing here?**

Mike: I was supposed to meet Ann.

Mari: **She was just here, but had to leave early.**

Mike: Did she say why?

Mari: **She said she had a new date.**

Mike: A new date?!

Mari: **But she was sorry** to miss **you.**

Mike: Oh, was she?

Mari: **You don't look *good.**

Mike: Really? I feel OK. What are you doing here anyway?

Mari: **Oh, just brushing up on my English.**

Mike: Let me see. Why don't I help you a little?

Mari: **Really? That's very kind of you.**

*good → well

茉莉：嗨！麥克。你在這裡做什麼？
麥克：我原本要和安碰面的。
茉莉：她剛剛還在這裡，不過有事必須先走了。
麥克：她有沒有說為什麼？
茉莉：她說她有了新的約會對象。
麥克：新的對象？！
茉莉：但是她很抱歉無法和你碰面。
麥克：哦！她會嗎？
茉莉：你看起來不太好。
麥克：是嗎？我覺得沒事。對了，你在這裡做什麼？
茉莉：噢！只是在加強我的英文。
麥克：讓我瞧瞧。我來幫你一下好了。
茉莉：真的？你真是太好了。

EXAMPLES... EXAMPLES... EXAMPLES...

- I'm sorry to have kept you waiting.
  我很抱歉讓你久等了。
- I'm sorry not to have telephoned.
  對不起我沒有打電話。
- She said she was sorry to have missed you.
  她說沒能見到你她覺得很遺憾。

...NOTES ...NOTES ...NOTES

表示「對做了～感到抱歉、遺憾」的心情時，用「I'm sorry to + have + 過去分詞」的句型。

miss 除了可解釋成「想念」之外，另外也有「錯過」的含意。

30 我可以去問別人。

I can ask somebody else.

Mari: **Excuse me, can you tell me where I can find this book?**

Clerk: Ah,...Western Economics...Cowboy stuff?

Mari: **I beg your pardon?**

Clerk: I just started working here. I don't really know that much.

Mari: **Oh. Well, if you can't help me I can ask somebody.**

Clerk: I am somebody! I'm just new, that's all.

Mari: **I'm sorry, my English is bad.**

Clerk: Your English is fine. It's my problem. Sorry I can't help you.

Mari: **That's OK. Thank you.**

茉莉: 對不起，您可不可以告訴我這本書在哪裡找得到？
店員: 呃，……西洋經濟學……牛仔類嗎？
茉莉: 請再說一次？
店員: 我剛到這裡工作，真的不知道那麼多。
茉莉: 噢！嗯！如果您無法幫我的話，我可以去問別人。〔問人〕
店員: 我就是人！我只不過是新來的而已。
茉莉: 對不起，我的英文不好。
店員: 您的英文很好。是我的問題。抱歉我幫不上您的忙。
茉莉: 沒關係的。謝謝您。

EXAMPLES… EXAMPLES… EXAMPLES…

- Do you want anything else?
  你還需要什麼其他的嗎？
- Your watch isn't here. It must be somewhere else.
  你的手錶不在這裡。一定是在其他地方。
- Who else shall we invite?
  還有誰是我們要邀請的？
- It's not mine. It's someone else's.
  那不是我的。是別人的。

…NOTES …NOTES …NOTES

else「其他的」，使用時接在以 some-, any-, every-, no- 開頭的字後面，例如 somebody else, anywhere else 等。另外也可以加在 what, who 等的疑問詞之後。

31

你看起來好疲倦，麥克。

You look terribly tired, Mike.

Mari: **You look terribly tiring, Mike. *What's wrong with you?**

Mike: Oh, hi, Mari. Do I look that bad? I'm sorry.

Mari: **No, I'm worried about you.**

Mike: Oh, I'm OK. I just didn't sleep last night.

Mari: **Why not?**

Mike: I was cramming for the test this afternoon.

Mari: ***I don't understand cramming.**

Mike: I'll explain it some other time.

Mari: **Mike, I'm very *boring.**

Mike: I don't think so. I think you're a nice person to be with.

Mari: **Huh?!**

*What's wrong with you? → What's wrong?

*I don't understand cramming. → I don't know what cramming means.

*boring → bored

茉莉：你看起來好疲倦，麥克。怎麼啦？〔你看來好無趣。
你是怎麼了？〕
麥克：哦！嗨！茉莉。我看來有那麼糟嗎？我很抱歉。
茉莉：沒有啦！我擔心你而已。
麥克：噢！我沒事。我只不過是昨晚沒睡。
茉莉：為什麼沒有？
麥克：為了今天下午的考試在臨時抱佛腳。
茉莉：我不懂 cramming 的意思。
麥克：我下次再解釋給你聽。
茉莉：麥克，我好無聊。〔我真是無趣〕
麥克：我不覺得。我覺得你是個很好相處的人。
茉莉：呵？！

EXAMPLES… EXAMPLES… EXAMPLES…

- The film was boring. I was so bored that I fell asleep.
  那部電影很無趣。我無聊得睡著了。
- The journey was very tiring.
  那次的旅行非常累人。
- I was surprised to get a prize —— but very pleased indeed.
  我很訝異得到獎 —— 不過真的非常高興。

…NOTES …NOTES …NOTES

形容詞中～ing 形式（現在分詞）表示「自動」；～ed 形式（過去分詞）表示「被動」。

因此 surprising, boring 便可解釋成事物「令人吃驚的」、「令人厭煩的」；而 surprised, bored 則是人「受驚的」、「（被煩得）感到生厭的」的意思。

32

我也不喜歡。

I don't like it either.

Mike: Boy, I'm hungry. Let's get something to eat.

Mari: **Yes, *I also.**

Mike: What would you like to eat?

Mari: ***Everything is fine.**

Mike: Oh, OK, well, then how about Italian? I don't like Japanese food.

Mari: **I don't like it** too。

Mike: Huh? I thought you said...oh, well...

Mari: **But no snails, please!**

Mike: OK, no snails. And no squid ink spaghetti. I don't like that.

Mari: **I don't *too.**

Mike: OK, let's go.

*I also → me, too
*Everything → Anything
*too → either

麥克：啊！我餓了。我們去吃點東西吧！
茉莉：好哇！我也是。
麥克：你想吃什麼？
茉莉：隨便。
麥克：噢！好，嗯！那義大利菜怎麼樣？我不喜歡吃日本料理。
茉莉：我也不喜歡。
麥克：呵？我以為你剛才是說……噢！算了……
茉莉：可是不要蝸牛，拜託！
麥克：好，不要蝸牛。還有不要烏賊墨汁義大利麵。我不喜歡那道菜。
茉莉：我也是。
麥克：OK，我們走吧！

EXAMPLES... EXAMPLES... EXAMPLES...

- I'm hungry. —— I am too./Me too./I am as well./So am I.
  我餓了。——我也是。
- I don't like Chinese food. —— I don't (like it) either./Me neither./Neither do I./Nor do I.
  我不喜歡中國菜。——我也是。

...NOTES ...NOTES ...NOTES

本課旨在說明「我也是」的用法。

表示認同、附和的 too, as well 到了否定句中必須改成 not... either, neither 或是 nor。

注意正確的語序是「So/Neither/Nor + 助動詞 + 主詞」。

33

希望會。

I hope so.

Mike: Excited about your first camping trip, Mari?

Mari: **Yes, very. I hope we see a bear.**

Mike: I don't know about that.

Mari: **Are you afraid, Mike?**

Mike: No, but I'm worried about the weather.

Jack: Hi Mari! Hi Mike!

Mike: Hi Jack! We're almost ready.

Jack: Mari, do you think it will clear up?

Mari: I'm afraid so.

Mike: Huh?

麥克：在為第一次的露營旅行興奮嗎？茉莉？
茉莉：是啊！非常興奮。我希望我們能看到熊。
麥克：那就難說了。
茉莉：你害怕嗎？麥克？
麥克：沒有，可是我擔心天氣。
傑克：嗨！茉莉。嗨！麥克。
麥克：嗨！傑克。我們快要準備好了。
傑克：茉莉，你覺得天氣會放晴嗎？
茉莉：希望會。〔我怕真的會〕
麥克：呵？

EXAMPLES... EXAMPLES... EXAMPLES...

- Do you think it will rain today? —— I hope not./I hope so./I'm afraid so.
  你覺得今天會下雨嗎？ —— 我希望不要。／我希望如此。／恐怕會吧！
- Is it too late for lunch? —— Yes, I'm afraid so. We're closed.
  已經過了午餐時間了嗎？ —— 是的，恐怕如此。我們關門了。

...NOTES ...NOTES ...NOTES

hope, be afraid 後面可以用 so, not 來避免內容重複，寫成 I hope so./I'm afraid not. 等簡短的句子。

think, believe 等的後面也是採相同的形式。

Is she English? —— I think so./I don't think so.

她是英國人嗎？ —— 我想是的。／我想不是。

34 我想凱文有信心獲勝。

I think Kevin is sure of winning.

Mari: **Wow! This is such a beautiful country!**

Mike: It is pretty, isn't it?

Jack: By the way, who's going to win the race next week?

Mari: **I think Kevin is** sure to win.

Kelly: I hope it's Steven. He's never won a race.

Mari: **Mike, please slow down.**

Mike: What's wrong, Mari?

Mari: **I'm *afraid to crash.**

Jack: Yeah, there's no hurry. Slow down, Mike.

Mike: OK, OK.

*afraid to crash → afraid of crashing

茉莉：哇！這個鄉村好美麗噢！
麥克：漂亮吧！
傑克：對了，誰會贏得下個禮拜的比賽？
茉莉：我想凱文有信心獲勝。
凱莉：我希望是史蒂芬。他一場比賽也沒贏過。
茉莉：麥克，拜託開慢一點。
麥克：怎麼了，茉莉？
茉莉：我怕會撞車。
傑克：是啊！不用急的。慢一點，麥克。
麥克：好，好。

EXAMPLES... EXAMPLES... EXAMPLES...

- George is sure to pass his exam.
  喬治一定會通過考試的。
- George is sure of passing his exam.
  喬治有自信考試能過關。
- I'm afraid to go out alone at night.
  我不敢一個人在晚上出門。
- We are afraid of missing our train.
  我們擔心會錯過火車。

...NOTES ...NOTES ...NOTES

表示「說話者」確信時，用 be sure to～「……一定會～」。

表示「當事人」確信時，用 be sure of～ing「……有自信會～」。

be afraid of～ing 「擔心會～」用於可能有事故發生時。

除了上述用法外， be afraid of～ing 還可以和 be afraid to「不敢～」互相替換。

I was afraid to tell [of telling] him the truth.

我不敢告訴他真相。

35

我希望凱莉沒有被吵醒。

I hope Kelly doesn't wake up.

Mike: Psst, Mari! Wake up!

Mari: **Wh...what is it, Mike?**

Mike: Remember you promised to get up early to make breakfast.

Mari: **Oh, yes, I forgot.**

Mike: Come on, I'll help you. Ahh....choo!

Mari: **Be quiet! I** don't hope **Kelly** wakes **up.**

Mike: OK, but you'd better hurry up. I'm hungry.

Mari: **Mike, the sky looks so dark. *I don't hope it rains.**

Mike: Ahh...me too, but anyway...I'll start peeling potatoes.

Mari: **I'll be out in a minute.**

*I don't hope it rains. → I hope it doesn't rain.

麥克：喂，茉莉！起來！
茉莉：什……什麼事呀！麥克？
麥克：別忘了你答應要早起做早餐的。
茉莉：噢！對了，我忘了。
麥克：來吧！我幫你。哈……啾！
茉莉：小聲點！我希望凱莉沒有被吵醒。
麥克：知道了，但是你最好快一點。我肚子餓了。
茉莉：麥克，天空看起來好暗。希望別下雨才好。
麥克：啊……我也希望，不過總是要……我去削馬鈴薯了。
茉莉：我馬上就出去。

EXAMPLES... EXAMPLES... EXAMPLES...

- I hope it doesn't rain.
  我希望不會下雨。
- I hope he won't be late.
  我希望他不會遲到。
- I hope you haven't been waiting long?
  我希望你不是等很久了吧？

...NOTES ...NOTES ...NOTES

在 I hope (that)...「我希望……」的句子中加入否定時， not 所修飾的必須是 hope 後面的動詞。

相反地，如果是 think, believe, suppose, expect 等其他的動詞，在否定時就必須寫成如同 don't think 等，以前面動詞為否定的形式。

I don't think she is English.

我不認為她是英國人。

36

我為你的成績感到難過。

I'm sorry about your results.

Mari: **Mike, you don't look happy. What's wrong?**

Mike: Didn't you see the exam results?

Mari: **Oh, that. I'm sorry for your results.**

Mike: I think you should be sorry for me.

Mari: **What?**

Mike: Oh, nothing. Hey, what about a game of catch with me and some of the boys?

Mari: **I don't know if I can do well.**

Mike: Oh, don't worry, it's easy.

Mari: **OK, I know. If I get the ball, I'll throw it *at you.**

Mike: No, please don't do that. I have enough problems.

Mari: **I don't understand.**

Mike: You throw the ball *to me* not *at me*...unless you are angry.

*at you → to you

茉莉: 麥克, 你看起來一臉的不開心。怎麼了?
麥克: 你沒看到考試成績嗎?
茉莉: 噢! 是那回事。我為你的成績感到難過。〔感到可憐〕
麥克: 我覺得你應該為我感到可憐。
茉莉: 什麼?
麥克: 噢! 沒什麼。對了, 你要不要跟我還有一些男生玩傳接球的遊戲?
茉莉: 我不知道我是不是可以做得好。
麥克: 噢! 別擔心, 很簡單的。
茉莉: OK, 我知道了。如果我接到球, 就把它丟給你。〔朝你丟〕
麥克: 不是, 千萬別那麼做。我問題已經夠多了。
茉莉: 我不明白。
麥克: 你要把球扔給 (to) 我, 不是朝我 (at) 扔……除非你生氣了。

EXAMPLES... EXAMPLES... EXAMPLES...

- I feel really sorry for John. He is terribly ill.
  我真為約翰感到難過。他病得好嚴重。
- I'm sorry about [for] losing your CD.
  我對弄丟你的 CD 感到抱歉。
- Can you throw my scarf to me, please?
  你可以把我的圍巾扔給我嗎? 拜託!

...NOTES ...NOTES ...NOTES

sorry for 用於表示「為人感到可憐」時; 如果對象指的是「事物」, 則必須改成 sorry about。

為「自己的行為」感到抱歉時, for/about 都可以使用。

throw 加上 to 表示投給對方的意思; at 則是瞄準後以對方為目標扔去, 帶有敵意的味道。

37

我到了之後會打電話給你的。

I'll phone you after I arrive.

Mike: Well, your plane leaves in 10 minutes.

Mari: **Thanks for driving me to the airport.**

Mike: Do you think your parents will be upset when you tell them about us?

Mari: **Don't worry, my mother will understand.**

Mike: It's your father I'm worried about.

Mari: **I'll phone you** after I will arrive.

Mike: Ahh..

Mari: **And you phone me before you *will leave for your home.**

Mike: I think my parents will be very happy.

Mari: **I'm *fearful to meet them.**

Mike: *Afraid*, Mari, but you don't have to be.

Mari: **See you soon, Mike.**

Mike: Bye, and good luck.

*will leave → leave
*fearful to meet → afraid of meeting

麥克: 嗯! 你的飛機在 10 分鐘後起飛。
茱莉: 謝謝你載我到機場。
麥克: 你想, 等你告訴你父母親我們的事, 他們會不會受不了刺激?
茱莉: 別擔心, 我媽會諒解的。
麥克: 我擔心的是你爸。
茱莉: 我到了之後會打電話給你的。
麥克: 呃……。
茱莉: 還有, 在回你家之前打個電話給我一下。
麥克: 我想我父母親會很開心的。
茱莉: 我不敢去跟他們見面。
麥克: Afraid, 茱莉, 不過你不用怕的。
茱莉: 再見, 麥克。
麥克: 再見, 祝好運。

EXAMPLES... EXAMPLES... EXAMPLES...

- I'll phone you before you leave.
  你出發之前我會打電話給你。
- Do come and see us when you're next in London.
  下次來倫敦時一定要來看我們。
- Let's wait until it stops raining.
  我們等雨停了再說。
- I'll call you as soon as I'm ready.
  等我一準備好就叫你。

...NOTES ...NOTES ...NOTES

when, before, after 等表示時間的連接詞後面, 即使接續的是「未來的事」, 也不可以用 will, 而必須使用「現在式」。

38

我叔叔建議我到銀行做事。

My uncle suggested that I get a job in a bank.

過了幾年，畢業即將來臨

Mike: Well, Mari, it won't be long before we graduate.

Mari: **Yes, Mike, I'm so *exciting.**

Mike: I think you mean *excited,* Mari.

Mari: **Oh, yes. Always the same mistake.**

Mike: What work are you planning on doing?

Mari: **My uncle suggested** me to get **a job in a bank.**

Mike: Is that what you want to do?

Mari: **Not really, but I don't know what to do.**

Mike: Have you ever thought of becoming a spy?

Mari: **A spy?! No, I never.....**

Mike: Well look here in today's paper.

Mari: **What is it?**

Mike: The CIA is recruiting college graduates.

Mari: **The CIA?**

 *exciting → excited

麥克：嗯！茉莉，再不久我們就要畢業了。
茉莉：是啊！麥克，我好興奮哦！
麥克：我想你是要說 excited，茉莉。
茉莉：噢！是的。老是同樣的錯誤。
麥克：你打算做什麼工作？
茉莉：我叔叔建議我到銀行做事。
麥克：那是你想做的嗎？
茉莉：也不是，但是我不知道要做什麼好。
麥克：有沒有想過當個間諜？
茉莉：間諜?! 沒有，從來沒……。
麥克：來看看今天報紙這裡寫的。
茉莉：什麼事？
麥克：CIA 正在招收大學畢業生。
茉莉：那個 CIA 嗎？

EXAMPLES... EXAMPLES... EXAMPLES...

- Jim suggested that we have [should have] fish for dinner.
  (=Jim said, "Let's have fish for dinner.")
  (=Jim suggested having fish for dinner.)
  吉姆提議我們晚上吃魚。
- She suggests we meet at the station.
  她提議我們在車站碰面。
- I suggested that she take a skiing holiday.
  我建議她去滑雪渡假。

...NOTES ...NOTES ...NOTES

表示「提議、建議」的 suggest 後面，美國通常是接續「that + 主詞 + 原形動詞」；英國則是用「that + 主詞 + should + 原形動詞」的形式。（另外也有 suggest～ing 的用法）

39

對不起，我沒帶。

Sorry, I haven't got one.

在冰淇淋店裡

Mari: **What are you reading, Mike?**

Mike: It's an application to join the CIA. Can you lend me a pen?

Mari: **Sorry, I haven't got** it。

Mike: Oh, then I'll do it later.

Mari: **Are you going to be a spy?**

Mike: I'm not sure, but it could be interesting.

Mari: **Can women join too?**

Mike: Sure, this is America, you know.

Man: Have you people decided yet?

Mari: **I'd like *big one with cream on it.**

Mike: I'll have a regular, please.

Man: We have a special Danish cheese special.

Mike: What do you say, Mari?

Mari: **I prefer French cheese to *Danish one.**

Mike: Ah, we'll pass on that today.

Man: Okey dokey.

*big one → a big one
*Danish one → Danish

茱莉：你在看什麼，麥克？
麥克：CIA 的報名表。你可以借我一支筆嗎？
茱莉：對不起，我沒帶。
麥克：噢！那我等會兒再做好了。
茱莉：你要去當間諜？
麥克：我還不知道，不過應該很有意思。
茱莉：女性也可以加入嗎？
麥克：當然，這裡是美國嘛！
店員：你們決定要點什麼了嗎？
茱莉：我要一個大的，上面有奶油的。
麥克：我要一個普通的，麻煩你。
店員：我們有特別的特製丹麥起司哦！
麥克：你說呢？茱莉？
茱莉：我偏愛法式起司，較不喜歡丹麥的。
麥克：嗯！我們今天不點那個。
店員：OK。

EXAMPLES... EXAMPLES... EXAMPLES...

- I haven't got an umbrella. I'll have to buy one.
  我沒有傘。我得去買一把才行。
  cf. Is that your umbrella? Can I borrow it?
  那是你的傘嗎？我可以借用嗎？
- I'm having a drink. Would you like one?
  我要喝杯酒。你要不要來一杯？
- Is this coat yours? —— No, mine is a grey one.
  這是你的外套嗎？ —— 不是，我的是灰色的。

...NOTES ...NOTES ...NOTES

one 的作用在於避免重複同樣的名詞。
當 one 的前面加有形容詞時，冠詞 a/an 不可省略。
複數形式的 ones 用於前面有 the 或是形容詞等修飾時。
one，ones 只能替代「可數名詞」使用。
Don't use powdered milk. Use this fresh (milk).
不要用奶粉。用這個鮮奶。

40

我恐怕兩天都不行。

I'm afraid neither day is possible.

Jones: Well, young Mari, I see you've done very well.

Mari: **Thank you, sir.**

Jones: What are your plans after graduation?

Mari: **I *don't decide yet.**

Jones: *Haven't*, Mari. *I haven't decided.*

Mari: **Oh, yes, thank you.**

Jones: We will be counseling next week.

Mari: **Yes, I heard.**

Jones: Can you come on Monday or Tuesday?

Mari: **I'm afraid** both days are not possible.

Jones: Well, then how about Thursday.

Mari: **That's OK.**

Jones: Will your parents be attending graduation?

Mari: **Unfortunately *none of my parents can come.**

Jones: *Neither*, Mari. *Neither of my parents.*

Mari: **Thank you, sir.**

*don't decide → haven't decided
*none → neither

瓊斯: 嗯！茉莉，我看你的成績非常好。
茉莉: 謝謝您，教授。
瓊斯: 畢業後的計畫是什麼？
茉莉: 我還沒決定。
瓊斯: Haven't, 茉莉。是 I haven't decided。
茉莉: 噢！是的，謝謝。
瓊斯: 下個禮拜要做諮詢。
茉莉: 是的，我聽說了。
瓊斯: 你可以星期一或星期二過來嗎？
茉莉: 我恐怕兩天都不行。〔兩天中只有一天可以〕
瓊斯: 嗯！那星期四怎麼樣？
茉莉: 那天可以。
瓊斯: 你父母會來參加畢業典禮嗎？
茉莉: 很可惜他們兩人都不能來。
瓊斯: Neither，茉莉。 Neither of my parents 才對。
茉莉: 謝謝您，教授。

EXAMPLES... EXAMPLES... EXAMPLES...

- Neither restaurant is expensive.
  兩家餐館都不貴。
- Neither of my sisters is [are] married.
  我的兩個姊妹都還未婚。
- Neither of us is [are] happy about the situation.
  我們兩人對這個情況都不開心。

...NOTES ...NOTES ...NOTES

「兩者皆為否定」時，用 neither 「（兩者中）沒有一個～是……」。

形式上可以寫成①「neither + 單數名詞」，②「neither of + the 等 + 複數名詞」或是「neither of + 代名詞」。

動詞須作單數。（口語中②的用法時，動詞常作複數）

none 是用於三者以上作否定時。

41

這輛車不值得修。

It isn't worth repairing the car.

Mari: **What are you doing, Mike?**

Mike: Well, I blew the gasket, so I'm replacing it.

Mari: **What's a gasket?**

Mike: Here, this thing here.

Mari: **How old is this car, Mike?**

Mike: Oh, only twenty years old.

Mari: **Twenty years old!?**

Mike: It's a great car, Mari.

Mari: **But you are always fixing it.**

Mike: Yeah, well, things happen.

Mari: **I think it isn't worth** to repair **the car, Mike.**

Mike: Oh, yes it is, Mari. They don't make cars like this anymore.

茉莉：你在做什麼，麥克？
麥克：嗯！墊圈爆裂了，所以我正在更換。
茉莉：什麼是墊圈啊？
麥克：這裡，就是這裡的這個東西。
茉莉：這輛車幾年了，麥克？
麥克：噢！才 20 年。
茉莉：20 年！？
麥克：這是一部好車，茉莉。
茉莉：可是你老是在修理。
麥克：是呀！嗯！難免的嘛！
茉莉：我認為這輛車不值得修，麥克。
麥克：噢！不，它值得的，茉莉。已經沒有人在生產這種車了。

EXAMPLES... EXAMPLES... EXAMPLES...

- It is really worth seeing the film.
  那部電影真的值得一看。
- It's not worth taking a taxi.
  不值得搭計程車前往。
- It's not worth discussing.
  這件事不值得討論。

...NOTES ...NOTES ...NOTES

It is worth～ing的句型意指「有做～的價值」。
也可以用「主詞 ＋ is worth～ing」，意思不變。
Those shoes aren't worth repairing.
那些鞋子不值得修理。

42

8 月見，如果我去紐約的話。

I'll see you in August if I come to New York.

Lady: Hello, CIA recruiting. May I help you?

Mari: **I am calling about your ad for recruits.**

Lady: Yes, well, we'll be holding interviews in New York during the month of August.

Mari: **Can anyone apply?**

Lady: If you are a U.S. citizen or hold a Green Card, you may apply.

Mari: **Yes, I have *Green Card.**

Lady: When will you be graduating, Miss?

Mari: **Hopefully in June.**

Lady: Do you want me to put your name down?

Mari: **Ahh, I have to check with my parents first, I think.**

Lady: OK, call us back when you've decided.

Mari: **OK, I'll see you in August** when **I come to New York.**

*Green Card → a Green Card

女職員：哈囉， CIA 招生部。有什麼我可以幫忙的嗎？
茉莉： 我打電話來詢問關於你們招生廣告的事。
女職員：是，好的，我們將在 8 月份於紐約舉辦面談。
茉莉： 任何人都可以申請加入嗎？
女職員：如果您是美國公民或是持有綠卡，您就可以申請。
茉莉： 有，我有綠卡。
女職員：您什麼時候畢業呢？小姐？
茉莉： 可望是在 6 月。
女職員：您要不要留個姓名？
茉莉： 呃！我想我得先和我父母商量。
女職員：OK，等您決定後再打電話給我們。
茉莉： OK，那 8 月見，如果我去紐約的話。

EXAMPLES... EXAMPLES... EXAMPLES...

- If Sue calls, tell her I've gone to the hairdresser's.
  如果蘇打電話來，告訴她我去美容院了。
- Stop talking when the bell rings.
  鈴響了就不要講話了。
- I will meet you when I next visit Paris.
  我下次去巴黎時會去找你。
- If (When) I eat too much, I get fat.
  如果吃的太多，我就會發胖。

...NOTES ...NOTES ...NOTES

「不確定是否會成真」時，用 if。

「確定會如此」、「看來將會成立」時，用 when。

表示真理或是任何時候都能成立的事情，兩者都可使用。
if=when, whenever.

43

要想通過考試，努力用功是一定要的。

To pass the test, you must do a lot of study

Mike: Hey, Mari. You are studying too much.

Mari: **No, Mike. To pass the test** a lot of study **must be done.**

Mike: Hmm. All work and no play makes Mari a dull girl.

Mari: **What do you mean?**

Mike: Nothing, nothing. Just an old proverb.

Mari: **I didn't understand this at all yesterday.**

Mike: Do you understand it now?

Mari: ***Not able to understand the problem alone, the teacher helped me.**

Mike: I see. Well, maybe we should work on your English a little.

Mari: **OK. Can you help me?**

Mike: Of course.

*Not able to understand the problem alone, the teacher～
→I wasn't able to understand the problem, so the teacher～

麥克：喂，茉莉。你太用功了。
茉莉：不，麥克。要想通過考試，努力用功是一定要的。
麥克：嗯哼！光是用功不玩耍，茉莉變成笨女孩
（好好學習亦應好好玩耍）。
茉莉：你的意思是說？
麥克：沒什麼，沒什麼。只是句老諺語。
茉莉：昨天我這題一點也不懂。
麥克：你現在懂了？
茉莉：我一個人是沒辦法，老師幫我的。
麥克：原來如此。嗯！也許我們應該用點心思在你的英文上。
茉莉：OK，你可以幫我嗎？
麥克：當然。

EXAMPLES... EXAMPLES... EXAMPLES...

- To replace the one he had lost, he bought a dictionary.
他買了本字典，用來彌補弄丟的那本。
- Reading my newspaper, I heard the doorbell ring.
就在看報時，我聽到門鈴響了。
- Without using a dictionary he translated the article.
他沒有用字典就翻譯好了那篇文章。

...NOTES ...NOTES ...NOTES

由分詞構句或是不定詞所引導的「真主詞」必須和「句子的主詞」互相一致，例如 To pass the test, you must do a lot of study. 一句中， pass 和do 的動作主體就同樣都是you。

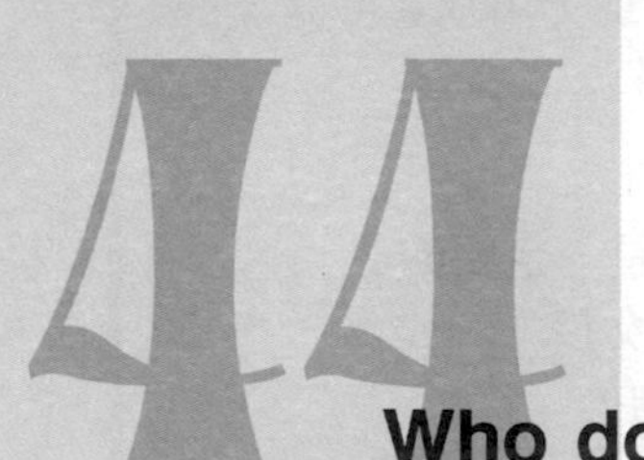

你想誰會贏?

Who do you think will win?

Mari: **What are you reading, Mike.**

Mike: Oh, hi, Mari. I was just reading the sports news.

Mari: **Do you think who will win Saturday's basketball game?**

Mike: Uhhh...the Bulls probably.

Mari: **Yes, I'm in love with Michael Jordan.**

Mike: I thought you were in love with me!

茉莉: 你在看什麼, 麥克?
麥克: 噢! 嗨! 茉莉。我不過是在看體育新聞而已。
茉莉: 你想星期六的籃球比賽誰會贏?
麥克: 呃……, 大概是公牛隊吧!
茉莉: 是啊, 我愛上麥可・喬丹了。
麥克: 我以為你愛的是我!

EXAMPLES... EXAMPLES... EXAMPLES...

- Who do you think invented the steam engine?
  你認為是誰發明了蒸氣機?
- Where do you think Tom has gone?
  你想湯姆去了哪裡?
  cf. Do you know where Tom has gone?
  你知道湯姆去哪裡了嗎?
- Who do you suppose telephoned today?
  你猜今天是誰打電話來?

...NOTES ...NOTES ...NOTES

在 do you think 與 who, what 等疑問詞連用的疑問句「你認為～?」的句型中, 疑問詞必須放在句首。其他同樣採取此類句型的動詞還有 guess, suppose, believe 等。

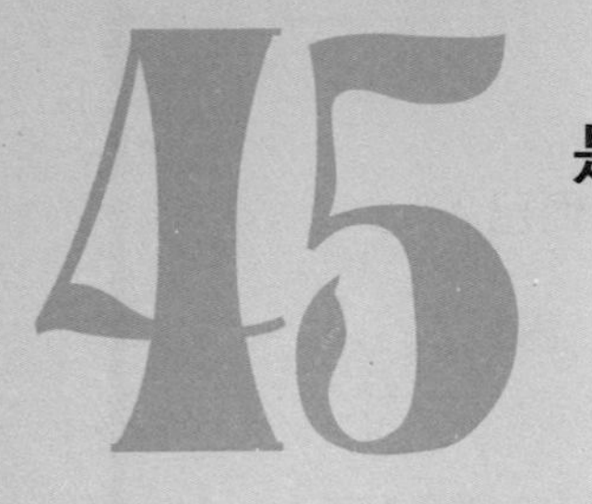

是呀！我還沒呢！

No, I haven't.

Mike: Haven't you written to your parents yet and told them we're getting married?

Mari: Yes, **I haven't.**

Mike: *No, I haven't,* Mari.

Mari: **You don't have to write to them, Mike. They don't understand English.**

Mike: I mean....oh, nothing, but I think you should write soon.

Mari: **OK, I'll write right now.**

Mike: Well, not that soon. Do you mind if I smoke?

Mari: ***Yes, please.**

Mike: Oh, OK, then. I won't.

Mari: **What?**

*Yes, please. → No, go ahead./Yes, I do.

麥克：你還沒寫信告訴你父母我們要結婚了嗎？
茉莉：是呀！我還沒呢！
麥克：No, I haven't 喲！茉莉。
茉莉：你不用寫信給他們，麥克。他們不懂英文的。
麥克：我的意思是……噢！沒什麼，不過我想你應該快點寫。
茉莉：OK，我現在馬上寫。
麥克：嗯！不用那麼快的。你介意我抽菸嗎？
茉莉：不會，請。〔是的，我介意。〕
麥克：噢！OK，那我就不抽了。
茉莉：什麼？

EXAMPLES... EXAMPLES... EXAMPLES...

- Didn't you go? —— No, I didn't.
  你沒去嗎？——是的，我沒去。
- You don't like milk, do you? —— Yes, I do. I love it./No, I'm afraid I don't.
  你不喜歡牛奶對不對？——不對，我喜歡。我愛死了。／對，我想我是不喜歡。
- You haven't seen John today, have you? —— No, I'm afraid not.
  你今天還沒看到約翰是不是？——是啊！恐怕還沒。

...NOTES ...NOTES ...NOTES

不論是肯定問句還是否定問句，只要「答案是否定」的，回答時一律用 No。

針對否定問句作答時，中文的「是的」等於英文中的 No。

Do you mind...? 也是一樣，回答 No 時，表示 I don't mind；回答 Yes 時，表示 I do mind。

Do you mind if I smoke? —— No, please do.

你介意我抽菸嗎？——不會，請抽。

46

我要去是因為我想去！

I'm going there because I want to!

Mike: Sure you want to meet my parents, Mari?

Mari: **Of course, Mike.**

Mike: You're not just being polite, are you?

Mari: **Mike! I love you!**

Mike: I love you too, Mari, but I'm worried.

Mari: **Why Mike?**

Mike: I just want to be sure that you are doing the right thing.

Mari: **I'm going there because I** want!

Mike: OK, I'm convinced. You're a tough cookie.

Mari: **Tough cookie?**

Mike: Nothing important.

麥克：你確定要去見我父母嗎？茉莉？
茉莉：當然囉！麥克。
麥克：你不會只是在客氣對不對？
茉莉：麥克！我愛你！
麥克：我也愛你，茉莉，可是我擔心。
茉莉：為什麼呢，麥克？
麥克：我只是要確定你這麼做是對的。
茉莉：我要去是因為我想去！
麥克：OK，我被你說服了。你這個難纏的小鬼。
茉莉：Tough cookie?
麥克：沒什麼。

EXAMPLES... EXAMPLES... EXAMPLES...

- You don't have to eat it if you don't want to.
  如果你不想吃，可以不要吃。
- Are you going to London next month? —— Well, I'd like to.
  你下個月要去倫敦嗎？——嗯！我是想去。
- Sue was planning to leave, but she's decided not to.
  蘇原先計畫要走的，不過她已經決定不走了。

...NOTES ...NOTES ...NOTES

to 不定詞的部分可以只保留 to，後面部分省略，以避免同樣字句重複。

want, like, try 的後面有時可連 to 也一起省略。

If you want, I'll go with you.

如果你願意，我跟你一起去。

47

這裡和花蓮一樣幾乎不下雨。

Rain here is as scarce as in Hualian.

Mike: Well, Mari, this is where I was born and grew up.

Mari: **It's so beautiful!**

Mike: Yes, it is nice here. But it's hot at this time of the year.

Mari: **I like the hot, Mike. Taiwan is also hot.**

Mike: Really? I've never been, so I can't imagine.

Mari: **And rain here is as scarce as** Hualian.

Mike: Hmm, yes, we don't get that much rain.

Mari: **And your parents are so nice and kind.**

Mike: They really like you, Mari.

Mari: **Mike, I'm so happy!**

麥克：嗯！茉莉，這就是我生長的地方。
茉莉：好漂亮！
麥克：是啊！這是個好地方。可是每年這個時候天氣很熱。
茉莉：我喜歡熱，麥克。臺灣也很熱的。
麥克：真的？我從沒去過，所以沒法想像。
茉莉：而且這裡和花蓮一樣幾乎不下雨。
麥克：嗯哼！是啊！這裡不怎麼下雨的。
茉莉：而且你的父母親人又好又慈祥。
麥克：他們真的喜歡你，茉莉。
茉莉：麥克，我好幸福喔！

EXAMPLES... EXAMPLES... EXAMPLES...

- The trains are more crowded at seven than at eight.
  火車在 7 點時比在 8 點時還要擁擠。
- The population of London is larger than that of Paris.
  倫敦的人口大於巴黎。
- Tom's salary is the same as mine.
  湯姆的薪水和我的一樣。

...NOTES ...NOTES ...NOTES

內文中作比較的雙方在中文是直接說成「這裡」和「花蓮」；換成英文時，則須考量雙方文法層級的一致性，寫成 "here" 對應 "in Hualian"。

48

我該用墨水筆還是用鉛筆填表？

Should I fill in the form in ink or pencil?

Lady: Next! Ah, Miss Mari Wang. So you want to join the CIA? Well, fill out this form, please.

Mari: **Should I fill it in with ink or pencil?**

Lady: *In* ink, Miss Wang. Next! Mr. Mike Bell.

Mike: Mari, they're calling me. 'Here's looking at you, babe.'

Mari: **Mike, stop talking *with that stupid voice.**

Mike: Hey, I'm just practicing being a spy, and it's *in* not *with*.

Mari: **By the way Mike, who's that man *with the funny hat over there?**

Mike: Oh, you mean the man *in* the funny hat. That's the famous Agent Tubs.

Mari: **What a funny hat!**

Lady: Last call for Mr. Mike Bell.

Mike: I'm coming!

Mari: **Mike, you are never *in time.**

Mike: Don't you mean *on time?*

*with that stupid voice → in that stupid voice
*with the funny hat → in the funny hat
*in time → on time

女職員: 下一位! 呀! 王茉莉小姐。這麼說您要加入 CIA 了嗎? 好, 請填好這張表格。
茉莉: 我該用墨水筆還是用鉛筆填?
女職員: 用墨水筆, 王小姐。下一位! 麥克・貝爾先生。
麥克: 茉莉, 叫到我了。「永誌不忘」。
茉莉: 麥克, 別用那種愚蠢的聲音講話。
麥克: 喂! 我只是在練習當個間諜; 還有, 是用 in 不是用 with。
茉莉: 對了, 麥克, 那邊那個戴著頂可笑帽子的人是誰? 〔帶著可笑帽子〕
麥克: 噢! 你說戴著那頂可笑帽子的人啊! 那是有名的泰伯幹員。
茉莉: 真好笑的帽子!
女職員: 最後一次叫麥克・貝爾先生。
麥克: 我來了!
茉莉: 麥克, 你沒有一次準時的。
麥克: 你是說 on time 吧!

EXAMPLES... EXAMPLES... EXAMPLES...

- We spoke in a low voice. (手段)
  我們小聲說話。
- Your boss is in a bad mood now. (狀態)
  你的老闆現在心情不好。
- She was dressed in a brown coat. (穿著)
  她穿著一件棕色外套。
- Shall we talk in private in my room? (情況)
  要不要到我房裡私下談談?
- We waited in a queue. (形狀)
  我們排隊等。
- Are we in time to catch the train? (時間)
  我們來得及趕上火車嗎?

...NOTES ...NOTES ...NOTES

本課旨在學習除了「地點」以外的 in 的用法。

Here's looking at you.

電影「北非諜影」中亨佛利・鮑嘉的一句著名對白。

49

你工作時都一定要穿黑西裝打領帶嗎？

Do you always have to wear a tie and black suit to work?

Mari: **Mike, I have a question *to you.**

Mike: *For you.*

Mari: **For me?**

Mike: I mean you should say, *I have a question for you.*

Mari: **Oh, I understand.**

Mike: Well, what is it?

Mari: Must **you always wear a tie and black suit to work?**

Mike: Well, this is the CIA. You know, MIB.

Mari: **MIB?**

Mike: Oh, nothing.

Mari: **By the way, you *don't have to tell Jack that we're getting married.**

Mike: Uh, what do you mean?

Mari: **He once asked me to be *his lover.**

Mike: Jack!? My old friend Jack?!

*to you → for you
*don't have to tell → mustn't tell
*his lover → his girlfriend（參見 23 頁 NOTES）

茉莉：麥克，我有一個問題要問你。
麥克：For you。
茉莉：For me?
麥克：我是說你應該說 I have a question for you.
茉莉：噢！我懂了。
麥克：嗯！什麼事？
茉莉：你工作時一定都要穿黑西裝打領帶嗎？
麥克：嗯！這就是CIA。你知道的嘛！ MIB。
茉莉：MIB?
麥克：噢！沒什麼。
茉莉：對了，你可不要告訴傑克我們要結婚的事。〔沒有必要說〕
麥克：呃！你的意思是？
茉莉：他曾經要我當他的女朋友。〔情人〕
麥克：傑克！？我的老朋友傑克？！

EXAMPLES... EXAMPLES... EXAMPLES...

- Must you really go so soon? Stay a bit longer.
  你真的需要這麼快走嗎？再待一會兒嘛！
- Do you always have to use the computer?
  你都一定得用電腦才行嗎？
- You mustn't do that.
  你可別那麼做。
- You don't have to do that.
  你沒有必要那麼做。

...NOTES ...NOTES ...NOTES

Must you～? 是用於詢問對方的意圖「一定要做～嗎」，通常是對方自己可以做的決定。

Do you have to～? 則是詢問「（義務上）必須要～是嗎」，經常用於已成立的「慣常的義務行為」。

You mustn't 是勸戒人「別做～」， You don't have to 則是告訴對方「沒有必要做～」的意思。

50

我搭往倫敦的火車幾點開?

What time does my train leave to London?

進入 CIA，坐在往歐洲的飛機上

Mari: **Mike, at what time does my train leave to London?**

Mike: I'm not sure. I thought you knew that.

Mari: **Oh, that's right...here's the schedule. Let's see, first the plane lands *in Frankfurt Airport, and...**

Mike: *At*, not *in*.

Mari: **Then we fly on to Paris and arrive *by 1p.m.**

Mike: *At*, not *by*. And then we wait, right?

Mari: **Our contact's arriving *by the 3:15 train on Austerlitz Station.**

Mike: *On*, not *by*, and *at* not *on!*

Mari: **Then we say goodbye and I take *the 7:00 train to London.**

Mike: *For*, not *to*.

Mari: **I hate prepositions!**

*in Frankfurt Airport → at Frankfurt Airport
*by 1p.m. → at 1p.m.
*by the 3:15 train on Austerlitz Station → on the 3:15 train at Austerlitz Station
*the 7:00 train to London → the 7:00 train for London

茱莉: 麥克，我搭往倫敦的火車幾點開?
麥克: 我不清楚。我以為你知道。
茱莉: 噢! 沒錯……行程表在這裡。我們來看看，首先飛機在法蘭克福機場降落，然後……
麥克: At，不是 in。
茱莉: 然後我們繼續飛到巴黎，在下午 1 點時抵達。
麥克: At，不是 by。接著我們開始等，對不對?
茱莉: 我們的連絡人會坐 3 點 15 分的火車到奧斯特里茨車站。
麥克: On，不是 by。還有是 at，不是 on!
茱莉: 然後我們道別，接著我坐 7 點鐘開往倫敦的火車。
麥克: for，不是 to。
茱莉: 我恨死介系詞了。

EXAMPLES... EXAMPLES... EXAMPLES...

- What time does the match start?
  比賽幾點開始?
- We arrived in Warsaw in the middle of the night.
  我們在半夜抵達華沙。
- Then I take the 6:20 train to Milano.
  然後我搭 6 點20 分的火車去米蘭。
- Then I take the 6:20 train for Milano.
  接著我搭 6 點20 分開往米蘭的火車。

...NOTES ...NOTES ...NOTES

What time 經常用來代換 when，雖然就文法規則而言， at what time 比較合理，但是在實際使用時，一般只用 what time，不加 at。

表示「旅行中的一個地點」、「等候會面的場所」等「狹隘的點狀空間」時，用 at。試比較 arrive at Paris「抵達巴黎」和 arrive in Germany「到達德國」的差異。

51 在郵局對面有一間茶館。

There's a tea house opposite the post office.

Tubs: Agent Wang, let's run through this one more time.

Mari: **Yes, Agent Tubs.**

Tubs: Go ahead and tell me what you're going to do.

Mari: **First I cross over to the kiosk and buy a paper.**

Tubs: OK, what next?

Mari: **The man will be sitting in a car parked before the post office.**

Tubs: *In front of*, not *before*.

Mari: **Yes, of course. And there's a tea house in front of the post office.**

Tubs: *Opposite*, not *in front of*.

Mari: **Yes, of course. I cross over to the tea house, stop, open up the paper before, no, in front of the car and then go inside and *drink for five minutes.**

Tubs: So far so good.

Mari: **A man will slip a coded message into my handbag.**

*drink for five minutes → have a drink and wait for five minutes

泰伯: 王幹員，我們從頭再來一次。
茉莉: 好的，泰伯幹員。
泰伯: 來吧！告訴我你要怎麼做。
茉莉: 首先，我走到對面的書報攤去買份報紙。
泰伯: OK，接下來呢？
茉莉: 那個人會坐在停在郵局前面的一輛車子裡。
泰伯: In front of，不是 before。
茉莉: 是的，當然。然後在郵局對面有一間茶館。
泰伯: Opposite，不是 in front of。
茉莉: 是的，當然。我走過去茶館，停下，在before，不對，是 in front of 車子打開報紙，然後走進去喝 5 分鐘飲料。
泰伯: 到目前為止還不錯。
茉莉: 一名男子會偷偷將一張密碼情報放進我的手提包內。

EXAMPLES... EXAMPLES... EXAMPLES...

- He lives in the house opposite mine.
  他住在我家對面的房子裡。
- The bank is opposite the station.
  銀行位於車站對面。
- Tom is sitting opposite Mary.
  湯姆坐在瑪麗對面〔的面前〕。
- There is a garden in front of the house.
  房子前面有座花園。
- He ran in front of the car and was knocked down.
  他跑到車子前面被撞倒了。

...NOTES ...NOTES ...NOTES

形容空間位置的 in front of「在～的前面」和opposite「在～的對面」，用法和中文相同。上述第 3 個例句:Tom is sitting opposite Mary. 湯姆坐在瑪麗對面，如果譯成「坐在瑪麗的面前」，則意思也有可能是 Tom is sitting in front of Mary. opposite 「面對面」的語意較不明顯，翻譯時最好避免。

in front of 和 before 意思同樣都是「在～的前面」，但是形容在建築物等「無生物」的前面時，通常是用 in front of。

52

您可以在星期五之前修好嗎？

Can you repair it by Friday?

Tubs: OK, Agent Wang, next you must go to the old watchmaker's on Bond Street.

Mari: **I think I know what I have to do.**

在鐘錶店裡

Man: Good morning, madam. What can we do for you, today?

Mari: **Well, I promised my husband to have this watch fixed for him.**

Man: I see.

Mari: **Can you repair it until Friday?**

Man: I think you mean *by* Friday, madam. And what time will he be returning, may I ask?

Mari: **He should be home *until five in the afternoon.**

Man: Don't you mean *by* five, madam?

Mari: **Oh, yes, of course. My English is *poorly.**

Man: *Poor*, madam, not *poorly*. Yes, very well. I'll have the package for you by then.

*until five → by five
*poorly → poor

泰伯：OK，王幹員，接下來你必須去一趟龐德街上的那間老鐘錶店。
茉莉：我知道我應該做什麼。

× × ×

店主：早安，女士。有什麼需要我為您服務的嗎？
茉莉：嗯！我答應我先生要替他拿這只錶來修。
店主：我懂了。
茉莉：您可以在星期五之前修好嗎？〔修到星期五〕
店主：我想您的意思是星期五之前 (by)，女士。我可以問一下您先生何時回來嗎？
茉莉：他應該會在下午 5 點前到家。〔會等到 5 點才回到家〕
店主：您是說 5 點前 (by) 吧！女士？
茉莉：噢！是的，當然。我的英文很破。
店主：Poor，女士，不是 poorly。是的，很好。我會在那之前替您包好的。

EXAMPLES... EXAMPLES... EXAMPLES...

- I'll be home by five o'clock.
  我會在 5 點以前回來。
- The photographs will be ready by Friday.
  照片會在星期五前弄好。
- Can I stay until the weekend?
  我可以待到週末嗎？
- I waited for her until 7 o'clock, and then left.
  我等她到 7 點，然後才離開。

...NOTES ...NOTES ...NOTES

by「在～之前」意指行動「發生在未來的某個時間點，或是更早之前」，不可以和 wait「等待」，stay「停留」等表示持續狀態的動詞連用。

反之 until，till「直到～（為止）」就是用於指「持續到某個時間點」的狀況或是狀態。

53 他長得什麼樣子？

What does he look like?

Tubs: Agent Wang, we're going to see how good you are at describing things.

Mari: **What should I do?**

Tubs: Go into the Ritz Hotel. One of the people is a Chinese spy.

Mari: **What does he look?**

Tubs: *Look like*, Agent Wang. That's your job to find out.

Mari: **Okay, Agent Tubs.**

Tubs: Then you should look around for the Russian spy.

Mari: **How does he *look like?**

Tubs: *Look!* And I don't know how he looks! But do you remember the secret words?

Mari: **"Ibiza *seems a nice place for a holiday."**

Tubs: *Seems like*, Agent Wang, *seems like!*

*look like → look
*seems a nice place → seems like a nice place

泰伯：王幹員，我們要來看看你描述事物的能力有多強？
茉莉：我應該做什麼？
泰伯：走進去麗池飯店。其中有一個人是中國間諜。
茉莉：他長得什麼樣子？
泰伯：Look like，王幹員。那就是你的工作去察覺了。
茉莉：好的，泰伯幹員。
泰伯：接著你要看看四周，找出俄國間諜。
茉莉：他看起來怎麼樣？
泰伯：Look！而且我不曉得他看起來怎麼樣！不過你記得暗語嗎？
茉莉：「Ibiza 似乎是個渡假的好地方。」
泰伯：Seems like, 王幹員，是 seem like!

EXAMPLES... EXAMPLES... EXAMPLES...

- How do I look? —— Very nice.
  我看來如何？——非常好。
- How's Mike? —— He's very well.
  麥克怎麼樣？——他非常好。
- How does he look? —— Not so well./Excited.
  他看來如何？——不太好。／興奮極了。
- What does he look like? —— Nice; like Al Pacino.
  他長得什麼樣子？——很好；像艾爾‧帕契諾。
- What is she like? —— She's tall and dark, and a bit shy.
  她人怎麼樣？——她高高黑黑的，還有點害羞。

...NOTES ...NOTES ...NOTES

How...?是用於詢問例如「心情、氣色」等「一時性變化的事物」。

What...like?則是針對「人的外在、個性」等較「固定不變的事物」來提問。

54

我想亞柏汀會贏。

I think Aberdeen will win.

Man: Hello, Pete's Pizza House.

Mari: **Hello? This is Agent Wang.**

Man: Yeah, well, what's your order?

Mari: **You are supposed to give me your code number.**

Man: You want my ID number?

Mari: **Yes, I think so...**

Man: Hold on,...OK, lady, it's 566672. Are you happy now?

Mari: **I'm not sure. OK, write this down.**

Man: It must be a big order.

Mari: **I think Aberdeen** wins.

Man: What?! Aberdeen never wins!

Mari: **I beg your pardon?**

Man: Lady, do you want some pizza or what?

Mari: **Uhh, I think I have the wrong number.**

店員：哈囉！皮特披薩店。
茱莉：哈囉？我是王幹員。
店員：是嘍！好哇！您要點什麼咧？
茱莉：你應該要告訴我你的密碼號碼的。
店員：您想知道我的身分證號碼？
茱莉：是的，我想是吧！
店員：等等，……OK，小姐，號碼是 566672。您現在高興了嗎？
茱莉：我不確定。好，把這個記下來。
店員：一定是個大訂單。
茱莉：我想亞柏汀會贏。
店員：什麼！亞柏汀才不可能贏咧！
茱莉：請再說一次？
店員：小姐，您到底要披薩還是要什麼？
茱莉：呃！我想我打錯了。

EXAMPLES... EXAMPLES... EXAMPLES...

- It will rain tomorrow.
  明天會下雨。
- She will be here in half an hour.
  她半小時內會到這裡。
- Do you think it will snow?
  你想會下雪嗎？
- You think we will succeed? —— Yes, probably.
  你想我們會成功？——是的，大概會吧！

...NOTES ...NOTES ...NOTES

對於未成定案，但是「預測將會發生」的事情用 will。因為是表示說話者的想法和推測，使用時經常與 think, believe, hope 之類的動詞或是 probably, perhaps 等一起出現。

55 她都作什麼打扮？

What kind of clothes does she wear?

Mike: Hello, Mari, is that you?

Mari: **Mike! I was just thinking about you.**

Mike: Well, I'm always thinking about you.

Mari: **Mike, I'm *embarrassing...where are you?**

Mike: I'm calling from the office in Paris. How is your training going?

Mari: **Oh, very well, I think. Agent Tubs is very patient with me. And you?**

Mike: Well, Agent Dubois is not so patient with me, but it's going well.

Mari: **What kind of clothes** is she wearing?

Mike: What?! I have no idea!

Mari: **What's wrong, Mike?**

Mike: Nothing really.

Mari: **Just two more months and then we can be together.**

*embarrassing → embarrassed

麥克: 哈囉! 茱莉是你嗎?
茱莉: 麥克! 我剛剛才在想你。
麥克: 哦! 我倒是無時無刻不在想你。
茱莉: 麥克, 我會害羞的……你在哪裡?
麥克: 我從巴黎辦公室打來的, 你的訓練進行得怎麼樣了?
茱莉: 噢! 非常順利, 我想應該是。泰伯幹員對我非常有耐心, 你呢?
麥克: 嗯! 杜鮑依幹員對我就沒那麼有耐心了, 不過進行得不錯。
茱莉: 她都作什麼打扮? 〔她現在穿什麼?〕
麥克: 什麼? 我一點也不清楚!
茱莉: 你怎麼了, 麥克?
麥克: 沒事, 真的。
茱莉: 再兩個月我們就能在一起了。

EXAMPLES... EXAMPLES... EXAMPLES...

- Where do you live? —— I live in Boston.
  你住在哪? —— 我住波士頓。
- I'm living in Oxford at present, but I haven't lived there very long.
  我目前住在牛津, 可是還不是住很久。
- You are being very quiet today.
  你今天非常安靜。

...NOTES ...NOTES ...NOTES

「表示狀態的動詞」通常不作進行式。
作進行式使用時, 有時候是指「一時性的狀態」。
Was she wearing earrings?
她那時有戴耳環嗎?

56

是啊！到 5 月此時，我就已經躺在沙灘上了！

Yes, this time in May, I'll be lying on the beach!

Tubs: Well, that's probably enough for today Agent Wang.

Mari: **Am I doing OK, Agent Tubs?**

Tubs: Better than most recruits, actually. How about a quick pint at the pub?

Mari: **I've never been inside a real English pub.**

Tubs: Well, what are we waiting for? Let's go.

在酒吧裡

Tubs: Cheers! Agent Wang.

Mari: **Cheers! Agent Tubs.**

Tubs: So, you are really determined to marry this Mike fellow in Paris?

Mari: **Yes, this time in May, I'm lying on the beach!**

Tubs: Hmmm...

泰伯：嗯！今天這樣大概差不多了，王幹員。
茉莉：我表現得好嗎，泰伯幹員？
泰伯：說實在地，比大多數新人還要好。要不要去酒吧喝點小酒呀？
茉莉：我從來沒去過真正的英國式酒吧！
泰伯：好，那我們還等什麼呢？走吧！

× × ×

泰伯：乾杯，王幹員。
茉莉：乾杯，泰伯幹員。
泰伯：這麼說，你真的決定要嫁給在巴黎的麥克同志了嗎？
茉莉：是啊，到 5 月此時，我就已經躺在沙灘上了。
泰伯：嗯……

EXAMPLES... EXAMPLES... EXAMPLES...

- David will be having dinner at 6 p.m.
  到下午 6 點時，大衛已經在吃飯了。
- This time tomorrow, I'll be sitting in the train to Prague.
  到了明天此時，我將會坐在往布拉格的火車上。
- Next summer John will be touring the United States.
  明年夏天時，約翰就已經在美國旅遊了。

...NOTES ...NOTES ...NOTES

表示「在未來某個時刻正在進行」的事，要用 will be～ing，並且必須加上如 this time in May 等表示未來時刻的提示。

（未來進行式也可以用於表示「情勢上必然將發生的行動」。）

I'll be meeting him.

我將會和他碰面。

HOUR

57

她就要生小孩了。

She's going to have a baby.

Mari: **Hello, Mike?**

Mike: Yes, hello? Mari? What time is it?

Mari: **I'm sorry to wake you up, Mike, but my mother just called from Taiwan.**

Mike: What happened? Is something wrong?

Mari: **No, it's my cousin. She'll have a baby!**

Mike: Your cousin is going to have a baby?

Mari: **Yes, going to have a baby!**

Mike: That's nice, but why did you phone me now?

Mari: **I feel so happy, Mike. Don't you?**

Mike: Ah, yes, of course. By the way, how's the weather in London?

Mari: **Let me look.....Mike, *it will rain.**

Mike: You mean *it's going to rain.* Well, that's London.

*it will rain → it's going to rain

茉莉：哈囉！麥克嗎？
麥克：是的，哈囉？茉莉嗎？現在幾點了？
茉莉：我很抱歉吵醒你，麥克，可是我媽剛從臺灣打電話來。
麥克：發生什麼事了？出了什麼事了嗎？
茉莉：不是的，是我表妹。她就要生小孩了。
麥克：你表妹就要生小孩了？
茉莉：對， going to have a baby!
麥克：那很好哇！但是你為什麼打電話給我呢？
茉莉：我覺得好開心，麥克。你會不會？
麥克：呃，會啊！當然。對了，倫敦的天氣如何？
茉莉：讓我看看……麥克，要下雨了。〔會下雨吧！〕
麥克：你是說要下雨了。嗯！那就是倫敦。

EXAMPLES… EXAMPLES… EXAMPLES…

- It's terribly cold. It's going to snow.
  天氣冷死了，就要下雪了。
- I feel terrible. I'm going to be sick.
  我覺得好難過，快要吐了。
- He's going to be late.
  他要遲到了。

…NOTES …NOTES …NOTES

be going to～除了有表示「打算要～」的用法外，另一個用法是表示「在極近的未來，或是眼前即將發生」的事情。後者的用法所依據的判斷理由是「由於其徵兆・趨勢・動機已經出現，所以認定一定會發生」，也就是「即將要～」的意思。

58

我明天要去巴黎看麥克。

I'm seeing Mike tomorrow in Paris.

Tubs: Agent Wang, today is shooting practice.

Mari: **OK, Agent Tubs, whatever you say.**

Tubs: Hold up your arms, take aim and bingo!

Mari: **Bingo?**

Tubs: That's just an expression. What are you doing this weekend, by the way?

Mari: **It's a long weekend, so I see Mike tomorrow in Paris.**

Tubs: Oh, is that so? What a terrible shame.

Mari: **What do you mean?**

Tubs: I might take you to Spain on a real assignment.

Mari: **Oh, that is very exciting, but what can I tell Mike?**

Tubs: Tell him it's business.

Mari: **OK, Agent Tubs, *I call you this evening.**

Tubs: *I'll* call you, Agent Wang.

Mari: **Oh, OK.**

*I call you → I'll call you

泰伯：王幹員，今天是射擊練習。
茉莉：好的，泰伯幹員，請吩咐。
泰伯：抬起你的手臂，瞄準目標，然後賓果（命中）！
茉莉：賓果？
泰伯：只是一種說法。對了，你這個週末打算怎麼過？
茉莉：這是個漫長的週末，所以我明天要去巴黎看麥克。
泰伯：哦！是那樣嗎？真是可惜。
茉莉：你的意思是？
泰伯：我說不定會帶你去西班牙執行一項真正的任務。
茉莉：噢！那真令人興奮，但是我要怎麼跟麥克說呢？
泰伯：告訴他這是工作。
茉莉：OK，泰伯幹員，我今晚打電話給你。
泰伯：I'll call you 才對，王幹員。〔我會打給你〕
茉莉：噢！好哇！

EXAMPLES... EXAMPLES... EXAMPLES...

- She is leaving for London tomorrow.
  她明天要去倫敦。
- When are you meeting John? —— I'm meeting him at 3 o'clock tomorrow.
  你何時要和約翰見面？ —— 我明天 3 點會和他見面。
- Are you having an interview tomorrow?
  你明天有面試嗎？

...NOTES ...NOTES ...NOTES

表示「已經確定要做的打算」時，用 be～ing，和另一個同樣表示意圖的 be going to～「打算要～」所不同的是，語感中多了「已經有了事前的準備、安排等」。

be～ing 適合用在說明個人性的預定計畫上。

59 他也許會帶我去西班牙。

He might take me to Spain.

Suzy: Hello, Mari. You've been busy lately.

Mari: **Hi, Suzy. Yes, and I was looking forward to the long weekend.**

Suzy: What do you mean 'was looking forward?'

Mari: **Well, Agent Tubs said that he will take me to Spain.**

Suzy: But I overheard the Director say that he might ask you.

Mari: **What's the difference?**

Suzy: Might means there's not much possibility.

Mari: **You mean I won't have to go?**

Suzy: Probably not.

Mari: **Thanks, Suzy, I feel better already.**

London

蘇西：哈囉！茉莉。你最近很忙喲！
茉莉：嗨！蘇西。是啊！我原先一直在期待這個長週末的。
蘇西：你說「原先一直」是什麼意思？
茉莉：嗯！泰伯幹員說他會帶我去西班牙。
蘇西：可是我聽說局長說他或許會問你。
茉莉：差別在哪兒呢？
蘇西：Might 是指可能性不大。
茉莉：你是說我不用去了？
蘇西：大概不用。
茉莉：謝了，蘇西，我已經覺得好點了。

EXAMPLES... EXAMPLES... EXAMPLES...

- I'm not sure yet but I may [might] go to Italy for my holidays.
  我還不確定，但是我說不定會去義大利渡假。
- It may rain tomorrow, but I hope it will be sunny.
  明天也許會下雨，但我希望會放晴。
- It might —— or might not —— rain.
  可能會 —— 也可能不會 —— 下雨。
- She might not come to the party because she's ill.
  她或許不會來派對了，因為她生病了。

...NOTES ...NOTES ...NOTES

說明某事「有可能發生」時，用 may, might「也許會～」。

這裡的 might 不是 may 的過去式，而是用來指未來的事，發生的可能性通常小於 may (50%左右)。如果改成用will，則是表示說話者確定會發生的可能性相當高。

It'll be windy tomorrow.
明天會起風。

60

到下個月就離開 5 年了。

I'll have been away for five years next month.

Tull: So, Agent Wang, I've been going over your report.

Mari: **Have I done something wrong?**

Tull: No, no, not at all. In fact quite remarkable.

Mari: **Thank you, sir.**

Tull: How long since you left Taiwan, now?

Mari: I'll be **away for five years next month.**

Tull: *Have been* away I believe.

Mari: **Thank you, sir. My English still needs much help.**

Tull: No, your English is fine. It says here you're planning on marrying Agent Bell.

Mari: **Yes, sir. We joined the agency together.**

Tull: Well, just don't let it interfere with your excellent work.

Mari: **Yes, sir, I mean no, sir.**

杜爾：嗯！王幹員，我已經看過你的報告書了。
茉莉：我什麼地方做錯了嗎？
杜爾：沒有，沒有，完全沒有。其實是非常優秀。
茉莉：謝謝你，長官。
杜爾：你離開臺灣多久了，到現在？
茉莉：到下個月就離開 5 年了。
杜爾：我想是 have been away 才對。
茉莉：謝謝你，長官。我的英文還須要多加強。
杜爾：不，你的英文很好。這上面寫說你打算嫁給貝爾幹員。
茉莉：是的，長官。我們一起加入情報局的。
杜爾：好，只要別因此影響到你的優異表現。
茉莉：Yes, sir，我是說 no, sir。

EXAMPLES... EXAMPLES... EXAMPLES...

- He will have left school by this time next year.
  明年此時他就已經離開學校了。
- By that time they will have forgotten you.
  到那時他們會已經忘了你。
- The exams will have finished by Thursday.
  考試會在星期四前結束。
- I'll have been living here for twenty years next year.
  到明年時，我就在這裡住了有 20 年。

...NOTES ...NOTES ...NOTES

說明在未來某個時刻之前「屆時～將會成立」，可以用「will + have + 過去分詞」或是未來完成進行式表示。

另外，未來完成式也可以用在說話者「有把握的推測」上。

He'll have arrived by now.

他現在應該已經抵達了。

61

我頭痛。

I have a headache.

Doc: Well, young lady, what seems to be the problem today?

Mari: **Thank you, doctor. I'm having a headache.**

Doc: A headache. And how long have you had it?

Mari: ***I've often got a headache, doctor.**

Doc: You often have headaches, you say?

Mari: **Yes, that's right.**

Doc: And what kind of work do you do, miss?

Mari: **Ahh, it's a secret, doctor. I cannot say.**

Doc: Well then perhaps stress is the problem.

Mari: **In Taiwan, stress is very *popular.**

Doc: Is it now? Anything else bothering you today?

Mari: ***I've been having a cold since Monday.**

Doc: You've had a cold, you say? Well that I can treat. Open up, say ahh..

*I've often got → I often get/have
*popular → common
*I've been having → I've had

醫生：嗯！小姐，今天的問題是？
茉莉：喔！醫生。我頭痛。
醫生：頭痛。有多久了？
茉莉：我經常頭痛，醫生。
醫生：您是說 you often have a headache?
茉莉：是的，沒錯。
醫生：您從事的是哪種工作，小姐？
茉莉：呃！那是個秘密，醫生。我不能說。
醫生：嗯！那麼也許問題是出在壓力上。
茉莉：在臺灣，壓力是很普遍的。〔很流行的〕
醫生：現在是這樣嗎？你今天還有沒有哪裡不舒服的？
茉莉：我從星期一感冒到現在。
醫生：您是說 you've had a cold 嗎？好，那個我有辦法治療。
把嘴巴打開，說啊……

EXAMPLES... EXAMPLES... EXAMPLES...

- I had an awful case of flu last week.
  我上星期得了重感冒。
- I've had a cold since Saturday.
  我從星期六開始就感冒了。
- I have an ache in my stomach.
  我胃痛。
- I have got a terrible headache.
  我頭痛很嚴重。

...NOTES ...NOTES ...NOTES

表示「生病了」時候的動詞用 have，雖然指的是現在進行中的事，但這裡的 have 不可以作進行式。

英式英語在口語中經常用 have got 代替 have，但是意思指的仍是現在而非現在完成。have got 一般也不用在表示反覆性動作、習慣等的事物上，所以不可以和 often 一起使用。

62

她幾分鐘前打過電話來。

She phoned a few minutes ago.

Mari: **Yes, hello? Department 443.**

Foot: Agent Sculder, please.

Mari: **She is out on assignment today.**

Foot: I see. Well then is Agent Tibbs in?

Mari: **Let me check, sir.....no answer from his extension.**

Foot: Well then how about Agent Fulder?

Mari: **Oh, she has phoned a few minutes ago, sir.**

Foot: She did, did she?

Mari: **Yes, sir, she did.**

Foot: Well how can I reach her?

Mari: **That's impossible, sir.**

Foot: Why is that?

Mari: **Because she is under deep cover.**

Foot: Yes, of course, well then, carry on, ahh, Agent...

Mari: **Wang, sir.**

Foot: Yes, Agent Wang.

茉莉：喂，哈囉？443 課。
孚特：請找史考德幹員。
茉莉：她今天出任務了。
孚特：是這樣子呀！嗯，那帝伯幹員在不在？
茉莉：我查查看，長官……他的內線沒有人接。
孚特：那麼福爾德幹員呢？
茉莉：噢！她幾分鐘前打過電話來，長官。
孚特：她打過，是嗎？
茉莉：是的，長官，她打過。
孚特：那我要怎樣才能連絡上她？
茉莉：那是不可能的，長官。
孚特：為什麼？
茉莉：她正深入地下工作中。
孚特：是啊！當然。嗯！那麼接下來，呃，幹員……
茉莉：王，長官。
孚特：是的，王幹員。

EXAMPLES... EXAMPLES... EXAMPLES...

- I got married a long time ago.
  我很久前結過婚。
- How long ago did it happen?
  那是多久前發生的？
- I saw him three days ago.
  我 3 天前見到他。
  cf. I saw him three days before the wedding.
  我在婚禮的 3 天前見過他。

...NOTES ...NOTES ...NOTES

ago「從今～以前」和過去式連用。
ago 不可以和過去完成式一起出現。
I've seen him before somewhere.
我以前曾在某個地方看過他。

63

我認識他很久了。

I've known him for a long time.

Suzy: I saw you talking to Agent Bell over there, Mari. Isn't he cute?

Mari: **Mike? Yes, I know him for a long time.**

Suzy: *I've known.*

Mari: **Yes, yes, I've known.**

Suzy: So you two are close?

Mari: **He's *my lover.**

Suzy: Shh! Don't say those things out loud, Mari.

Mari: **Did I say something wrong?**

Suzy: Well, no, but...

Mari: **We are getting married after our training is over.**

Suzy: Really? That's wonderful!

*my lover → my boyfriend/fiancé (參見 23 頁 NOTES)

蘇西：我看到你和貝爾幹員在那邊說話，茉莉。
　　　你看他是不是很可愛？
茉莉：麥克？是啊！我認識他很久了。
蘇西：I've known 吧！
茉莉：對，對， I've known.
蘇西：你們兩個人很親密？
茉莉：他是我的男朋友。〔情夫〕
蘇西：噓！那種事別大聲嚷嚷，茉莉。
茉莉：我說了不該說的事了嗎？
蘇西：嗯！沒有，不過……。
茉莉：我們打算訓練結束後就結婚。
蘇西：真的？那太好了！

EXAMPLES... EXAMPLES... EXAMPLES...

- How long have you known Mike?—— I've known him since 1993.
  你認識麥克多久了？——我從 1993 年開始跟他認識的。
- I've always liked you.
  我原本一直喜歡你。
- How long have you been married?—— For ten years.
  你（們）結婚多久了？——有 10 年了。
- I have smoked since I was eighteen.
  我從 18 歲開始抽菸。

...NOTES ...NOTES ...NOTES

說明「至今有一段時日的事」時，可以用表示期間的片語 (for～, since～等)加上「 have ＋ 過去分詞」的句型。

64 貝爾幹員摔斷了他的腿。

Agent Bell has broken his leg.

執行在中美洲的任務

Mari: **Come in 338, this is Agent Wang with Agent Bell. Over.**

Man: 338 here. You're coming in clear, Agent Wang. Over.

Mari: **We have the drug dealers covered, but Agent Bell broke his leg. Over.**

Man: Leave him. Someone will get him later. Over.

Mari: **I understand. Over and out.**

Mari: Mike, I have to leave you.

Mike: It's standard procedure. I understand.

Mari: **Mike, you *were the best man for me.**

Mike: What? Are you going to shoot me?

Mari: **What?! No! I just don't want to leave you.**

Mike: I know that, but the mission is more important than our love.

Mari: **You're right. I have to go. Good bye, Mike.**

*were → are

茱莉: 呼叫 338, 這裡是王幹員和貝爾幹員。完畢。
男子: 這裡是 338。你們的收訊良好, 王幹員。完畢。
茱莉: 我們掌握了毒販的行蹤, 可是貝爾幹員摔斷了他的腿。完畢。
男子: 留下他。有人會去接應他的。完畢。
茱莉: 知道了。通話結束。
茱莉: 麥克, 我必須留下你。
麥克: 那是標準的程序。我了解。
茱莉: 麥克, 你是我最好的伴侶。〔你曾經是……〕
麥克: 什麼? 你打算槍殺我嗎?
茱莉: 什麼?! 不! 我只是不想留下你。
麥克: 我知道, 可是任務比我們的感情還重要。
茱莉: 你說得對。我必須走了, 再見, 麥克。

EXAMPLES... EXAMPLES... EXAMPLES...

- Meg isn't here. She's gone shopping.
  梅格不在。她去買東西了。
- I have finished "Ulysses." What shall I read now?
  我讀完了《尤利西斯》。現在讀什麼好呢?
- Have you ever been to Hawaii?—— Yes, twice.
  你去過夏威夷嗎? ——是的, 去過兩次。
- It has snowed every winter for years.
  已經好多年每年冬天都下雪了。

...NOTES ...NOTES ...NOTES

「have + 過去分詞」意指過去的事以某種的形式和現在產生關連, 主要用於「說明～至今發生過幾次」或是「認為目前的情形是過去行為所導致的結果」時。

65

我想起我以前見過他。

I realized that I had seen him before.

Man: So how did you know that he was the man?

Mari: **Well, a week ago in the hotel lobby.....**

Man: Yes, what?

Mari: **I noticed a man acting strangely.**

Man: Hmm...

Mari: **And then yesterday at the stakeout, I felt very strange.**

Man: Why was that?

Mari: **Well, I realized that I saw him before.**

Man: *Had, seen.*

Mari: **Yes, had seen... well, it was the man from the hotel lobby.**

Man: The same man? Are you sure?

Mari: **Yes, he was the same man, sir.**

男子：所以你怎麼知道他就是那個男人？
茉莉：嗯！一個星期前在旅館大廳……
男子：是，然後？
茉莉：我注意到一個男人鬼鬼祟祟的。
男子：嗯哼……
茉莉：然後昨天在盯哨時，我覺得非常奇怪。
男子：怎麼了？
茉莉：嗯！我想起我以前見過他。
男子：Had seen。
茉莉：是的，had seen...嗯！那正是旅館大廳的那個男人。
男子：同一個男人？你確定？
茉莉：是的，他就是同一個男人，長官。

EXAMPLES... EXAMPLES... EXAMPLES...

- When I arrived, Tom had already gone home.
  當我抵達時，湯姆已經回家了。
- He told me he had met me when I was young.
  他告訴我他在我年輕時曾經遇見我。
- The boys loved the zoo. They had never seen wild animals before.
  男孩子們愛極了動物園。他們之前從沒見過野生動物。

...NOTES ...NOTES ...NOTES

使用「had＋過去分詞」可以明確表現出過去發生的兩件事情在「時間上的前後關係」，其中較早發生的一方用的是過去完成式。

66

這是我第一次看歌劇。

This is the first time I've come to the opera.

觀賞歌劇

Suzy: Well, Mari, are you excited?

Mari: **I am *too excited.**

Suzy: Hey, relax, it's just the opera.

Mari: **But this is the first time I came to the opera!**

Suzy: But it hasn't even started yet!

Mari: **By the way, how is Stuart?**

Suzy: We broke up two months ago.

Mari: **I'm sorry.**

Suzy: Don't be, I'm not. I'm in love again!

Mari: **Again?! Oh! *Surprise!**

Suzy: What?

Mari: **So this is the third time you *were in love this year!**

Suzy: Actually it's the fifth, but so what?

*too excited → so excited
*Surprise! → What a surprise!
*were → have been

蘇西：嗯！茉莉，你興奮嗎？
茉莉：我太興奮了。
蘇西：喂，放輕鬆，這只是歌劇而已。
茉莉：可是這是我第一次看歌劇嘛！
蘇西：但是甚至都還沒開始呢！
茉莉：對了，史都特好嗎？
蘇西：我們兩個月前分手了。
茉莉：我很抱歉。
蘇西：用不著，我可不覺得。我又戀愛了！
茉莉：又?！噢！真是驚人！
蘇西：什麼嘛？
茉莉：這是你今年第三次戀愛了吔！
蘇西：其實是第五次，但是那又怎樣？

EXAMPLES... EXAMPLES... EXAMPLES...

- This is the first time he has driven a car.
  這是他第一次開車。
- Is this the first time you've been to England?
  這是你第一次來英國嗎？
  —— Yes, I've never been to England before.
  —— 是的，我以前從沒來過英國。
- She's the most interesting person I've ever met.
  她是我遇過最有意思的人。
- He's lost his passport again. It's the second time he has lost it.
  他又弄丟了他的護照。這已經是第二次了。

...NOTES ...NOTES ...NOTES

This [That, It] is the first [second, only, best, most interesting 等]～的後面，要用現在完成式。

67

如果他有足夠的錢，他會買一棟。

He would buy one if he had enough money.

在開車的路上

Suzy: So, Mari, have you and Mike decided where to settle down eventually?

Mari: **We were looking at some magazines yesterday. Houses in Hawaii.**

Suzy: But they are so expensive!

Mari: **Mike says he will buy one if he has enough money.**

Suzy: Didn't he say *would* if he *had?*

Mari: **Uhh, yes, maybe he did.**

Suzy: They're quite different you know.

Mari: **What's that noise?**

Suzy: It's an Italian car, you know.

Mari: **Does it always make that noise.**

Suzy: No, actually that was the first time.

Mari: ***If I am you, I will get this car serviced.**

 *If I am you, I will get → If I were you, I would get

蘇西：對了，茉莉，你和麥克最後決定要在哪裡定居了嗎？
茉莉：我們昨天看了一下雜誌。在夏威夷的房子。
蘇西：但是那很貴吔！
茉莉：麥克說如果錢夠了，他會買一棟。
蘇西：他該不是說如果他有的話 (had) 他會 (would) 吧？
茉莉：呃！對，也許是。
蘇西：這兩句話是非常不同的，你知道吧！
茉莉：那是什麼聲音？
蘇西：這是部義大利車，你知道的。
茉莉：它常常會發出那種聲音嗎？
蘇西：不會，其實剛剛那是第一次。
茉莉：如果我是你，我會把這輛車送修。

EXAMPLES... EXAMPLES... EXAMPLES...

- If I found $100 in the street, I would keep it.
  如果我在路上發現了 100元，我會自己留起來。
- What would you do if you won a million pounds?
  如果你贏得 100 萬英鎊的話，你會怎麼做？
- If I were you, I'd take up a sport to keep fit.
  如果我是你，我會做運動保持身材。

...NOTES ...NOTES ...NOTES

針對「多半不會發生的事」或者「只是單純假想的狀況」，要用假設語氣。因此儘管舉的例子是「現在的事、今後的事」，正確用法必須要改成過去式。（如果是普通的現在式 if 條件句，則意指所舉的例子有實現的可能）

If I were you, I would～可以理解為「要是我的話會做～（你也照做吧）」的建議句。

68

她早該去看醫生的。

She should have seen a doctor.

Mike: Hello, Mari, it's me, Mike.

Mari: **Oh, Mike. How are you?**

Mike: Fine, sweetie, how are you?

Mari: **Not so good.**

Mike: How come?

Mari: **It's Suzy, my new roommate.**

Mike: What's wrong?

Mari: **She hasn't been feeling very well.**

Mike: Has she seen a doctor?

Mari: **No. She** must have seen **a doctor when she first fell ill, but she didn't.**

Mike: Well, you have to do something.

Mari: **OK, Mike. I'll call the doctor right away.**

麥克：哈囉！茱莉，是我麥克。
茱莉：噢！麥克。你好嗎？
麥克：很好，親愛的，你呢？
茱莉：不太好。
麥克：怎麼會？
茱莉：因為蘇西，我的新室友。
麥克：怎麼了？
茱莉：她身體一直不太好。
麥克：她去給醫生看了嗎？
茱莉：沒有。她在一開始覺得不舒服時，就該去看醫生的，可是她沒有。
麥克：嗯！你必須做點什麼。
茱莉：知道了，麥克。我會馬上打電話給醫生的。

EXAMPLES... EXAMPLES... EXAMPLES...

- You should have gone to the dentist yesterday.
  你昨天應該去看牙醫的。
- I should have left Paris before 6, but I didn't.
  我應該在 6 點前離開巴黎的，但是我沒有。
- I'm feeling sick. I shouldn't have eaten so much chocolate.
  我覺得不舒服。我不該吃那麼多巧克力的。

...NOTES ...NOTES ...NOTES

表示「當時應該～的」該做而未做的事情時，要用「should+have+過去分詞」的句型。

「must+have+過去分詞」意思是指「一定（已經）～了」的推測。

It's 9:30. He must have arrived at the office by now.
9 點半了。他現在一定已經到公司了。

69

跟你一起坐在這裡蠻好的。

It's nice to be sitting with you here.

Suzy: Mari, thanks for calling the doctor.

Mari: **I *should call much earlier. I'm sorry.**

Suzy: I don't like doctors or hospitals, really.

Mari: **But you must take care of *your body.**

Suzy: *Yourself*, Mari, not *your body*.

Mari: **Oh.**

Suzy: But you don't have to stay here with me. I know you're busy.

Mari: **No, it's nice to sit with you here.**

Suzy: Oh, you are a darling, aren't you?

Mari: **I know what it's like to be sick.**

Suzy: Well, the doctor said it wasn't serious.

Mari: **You'll be *good very soon.**

Suzy: *Better*, Mari, *better*.

Mari: **Oh, yes. You're right.**

*should call → should have called
*your body → yourself
*good → better

蘇西：茉莉，謝謝你叫醫生來。
茉莉：我應該更早叫的。對不起。
蘇西：我不喜歡醫生或是醫院，真的。
茉莉：可是你得照顧你自己的身體。〔自己的軀體〕
蘇西：Yourself，茉莉，不是 your body。
茉莉：噢！
蘇西：不過你不用待在這裡陪我的，我知道你很忙。
茉莉：不會的，跟你一起坐在這裡蠻好的。
蘇西：噢！你真好，不是嗎？
茉莉：我知道生病是什麼感受。
蘇西：嗯！醫生說並不嚴重。
茉莉：你很快就會好起來的。
蘇西：Better，茉莉，是 better。
茉莉：噢！是的。你說得對。

EXAMPLES... EXAMPLES... EXAMPLES...

- He seems to be living around here.
  他好像就住在這附近。
- He seems to be smoking a lot.
  他似乎菸抽得很凶。
- He appears to be waiting for someone.
  他一副在等人的樣子。
- I happened to be standing next to him when he collapsed.
  當他倒下時，我正好站在他旁邊。

...NOTES ...NOTES ...NOTES

表示「狀態」的動詞（live, sit, lie, stand 等）作進行式用時，強調的是「暫時的狀態」或「情感的鮮活」表達。

70

真希望我的記憶力好一點！

I wish I had a better memory!

Tubs: Agent Wang, I'll go through it once more.

Mari: **Yes, Agent Tubs, I'm ready.**

Tubs: OK. If he nods to the left, the meeting is off.

Mari: **The meeting is off.**

Tubs: If he nods to the right, the meeting is postponed.

Mari: **The meeting is postponed.**

Tubs: If he nods up and to the left, the meeting is on Tuesday.

Mari: **Meeting on Tuesday.**

Tubs: If he nods down and to the right, the meeting is on Thursday.

Mari: **Meeting on Thursday.**

Tubs: If he shakes his left leg, the meeting.....

Mari: **Oh, I wish I have a better memory!**

Tubs: *Had*, Agent Wang, *had!*

泰伯：王幹員，我再做一次。
茱莉：是，泰伯幹員，我準備好了。
泰伯：OK。如果他頭向左點，會議就結束。
茱莉：會議結束。
泰伯：如果他頭向右點，會議延期。
茱莉：會議延期。
泰伯：如果他頭朝左上方點，會議就在星期二。
茱莉：會議在星期二。
泰伯：如果他頭朝右下方點，會議就在星期四。
茱莉：會議在星期四。
泰伯：如果他搖動左腿，會議……
茱莉：噢！真希望我的記憶力好一點！
泰伯：Had，王幹員，是had！

EXAMPLES... EXAMPLES... EXAMPLES...

- I wish I knew his address.
  但願我知道他的住址。
- I wish I were a millionaire.
  要是我是個百萬富翁那該多好。
- It's snowing. I wish it wasn't snowing.
  下雪了。要是沒下雪就好了。
- Do you ever wish you could fly?
  你曾經希望你能飛嗎？

...NOTES ...NOTES ...NOTES

當現實「不符合自己所期望」時，可以用「wish 後面接主詞＋過去式」（假設語氣過去）來表現說話者「遺憾的心情」。

71

這輛車聽起來聲音有點怪。

The car sounds a bit funny.

Mari: **Morning, Agent Morgan, you're new, right?**

Morgan: Yes, Agent Wang, I just joined the agency.

Mari: **Well, today we have to drive to a pickup.**

Morgan: Yes, Agent Wang. Let's go.

Mari: **The car is sounding a bit funny.**

Morgan: But it *was sounding like this yesterday, too.

Mari: **We should have it serviced right away.**

Morgan: Whatever you say.

Mari: **What are you doing, Agent Morgan?**

Morgan: I'm smelling my shirt to see if I can wear it for another day.

Mari: **I think you should wash it.**

Morgan: Yes, Agent Wang.

Mari: **And I think you should have this car cleaned, inside and out.**

Morgan: What's wrong, Agent Wang?

Mari: **It *smells rotten fish!**

*was sounding → sounded
*smells rotten fish → smells of rotten fish

茉莉：早，摩根幹員，你是新來的，對吧？
摩根：是的，王幹員，我剛加入情報局。
茉莉：嗯！今天我們必須開車去回收情報。
摩根：是，王幹員。我們走吧！
茉莉：這輛車聽起來聲音有點怪。
摩根：但是它昨天聽起來也是這個聲音。
茉莉：我們應該馬上送修。
摩根：遵命。
茉莉：你在做什麼，摩根幹員？
摩根：我在聞我的襯衫，看看是否可以再穿一天。
茉莉：我覺得你該洗一洗了。
摩根：是，王幹員。
茉莉：還有我想你該清理這輛車了，裡外都要。
摩根：有什麼問題嗎，王幹員？
茉莉：它聞起來像條臭掉了的魚！

EXAMPLES... EXAMPLES... EXAMPLES...

- Pete sounded angry when I spoke to him on the phone.
  我和皮特通話時，他的聲音聽起來像是在生氣。
- The dinner smells good.
  晚餐聞起來好香。
- She sounds like an actress.
  她講起話來像個女演員。
- Her hands smelled of fish.
  她的手有魚腥味。
- Why are you smelling the meat? Has it gone bad?
  你為什麼要聞這肉？壞掉了嗎？

...NOTES ...NOTES ...NOTES

感官動詞（sound, smell, taste 等）後面用的如果是形容詞，此時通常不用進行式。sound 表示「發出～似的聲音」、「聽起來像～」；smell 則是「聞起來～」的意思。

另外也可以寫成「sound like/smell of [smell like] + 名詞」的形式。

smell 如果作「嗅」的動作解釋時，便可以用進行式作表示。

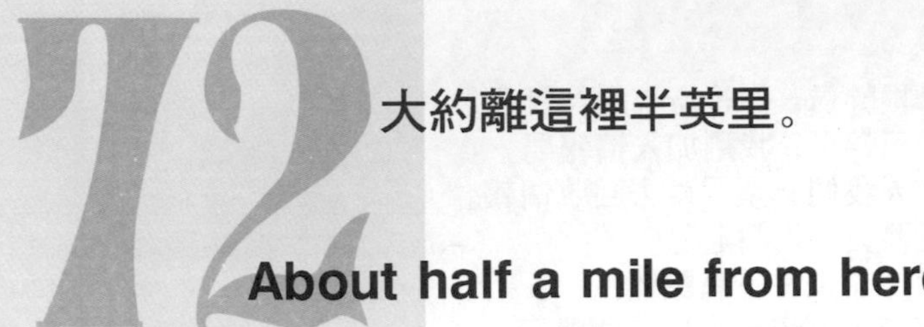

72 大約離這裡半英里。

About half a mile from here.

執行新任務

Tubs: Hello, Agent Wang. Come in. Over.

Mari: **Hello, this is Agent Wang. Over.**

Tubs: What's your position? Over.

Mari: **I've been waiting for *one and a half hour. Over.**

Tubs: What is the suspect doing? Over.

Mari: **He has gone into the same shop several times. Over.**

Tubs: Where is the shop? Over.

Mari: **About** half of a mile **from here. Over.**

Tubs: We'll send some more agents. Over.

Mari: **I'll wait here. Over.**

Tubs: Don't let him see you. Over and out.

*one and a half hour → one and a half hours

泰伯: 哈囉，王幹員。收到請講，完畢。
茉莉: 哈囉，這裡是王幹員，完畢。
泰伯: 你現在的情況如何？完畢。
茉莉: 我已經等了一個半小時了。完畢。
泰伯: 嫌犯正在做什麼？完畢。
茉莉: 他在同一家店進出了好幾次。完畢。
泰伯: 店的位置在哪裡？完畢。
茉莉: 大約離這裡半英里。完畢。
泰伯: 我們會多派一些幹員過去的。完畢。
茉莉: 我會在這裡待命。完畢。
泰伯: 別讓他看到你，通話結束。

EXAMPLES... EXAMPLES... EXAMPLES...

- I'm leaving in half an hour.
  我在 30 分鐘內要出發。
- I've been waiting for one and a half hours.
  我已經等了一個半小時了。
- One and a half kilos of sugar, please.
  請給我 1 公斤半的砂糖。

...NOTES ...NOTES ...NOTES

當 half 和 mile, dozen 等「量詞」一起出現時，不可以作 half of 的形式，正確用法是說成 half a dozen 「半打」，half a dollar「半美元」，half a pint (of milk)「半品脫的牛奶」。

（cf. half (of) the money「那些錢的一半」，half (of) these apples「那些蘋果的一半」）

另外，像是 one and a half, two and a half 等加了數量的名詞，後面所銜接的量詞也必須改作複數，如 miles, hours 等。（帶有分數、小數的名詞一般被視為複數）

73

我等了你們好久。

I waited a long time for you.

Tubs: Agent Wang, are you there?

Mari: **Over here. What took you so long?**

Tubs: I had a flat tire. I'm sorry.

Mari: I waited long **for you.**

Tubs: Well, where is the suspect?

Mari: **He's over in that green house over there.**

Tubs: OK, then stay here and cover us. We're going in.

Mari: **Good luck.**

泰伯：王幹員，你在那裡嗎？
茉莉：在這兒。你們怎麼這麼久？
泰伯：我輪胎沒氣了。真是抱歉。
茉莉：我等了你們好久。
泰伯：嗯！嫌犯在哪裡？
茉莉：他在對面那棟綠色的房子裡。
泰伯：OK，那麼你留在這裡掩護我們。我們要衝進去了。
茉莉：祝你們好運。

EXAMPLES... EXAMPLES... EXAMPLES...

- Have you been waiting long?
  你等了很久嗎？
  —— No, not long. Only two or three minutes.
  沒有，不久。只有 2、3 分鐘。
  —— A long time. More than half an hour.
  很久。超過半小時了。
- We have known each other for a long time.
  我們認識彼此有好長一段時間了。
- Sorry I've kept you waiting so long.
  抱歉我讓你等了那麼久。

...NOTES ...NOTES ...NOTES

long 在肯定句中出現時，通常作 (for) a long time。

long 單獨出現時，通常是在疑問句、否定句中。

long 用於肯定句時，通常不是在前面加上 so, too，就是在後面加 enough, ago, before 等。

74 你們走了多遠呢？

How far did you walk?

Mari: **Agent Tubs, you look very tiring, I mean tired.**

Tubs: Yes, well, it was quite a long walk.

Mari: **How long did you walk?**

Tubs: About one hour.

Mari: **Huh?**

Tubs: But we caught the man we were after.

Mari: **Yes, the director will be happy.**

Tubs: You did a good job, Agent Wang.

Mari: **Thanks to you, Agent Tubs.**

茉莉：泰伯幹員，你看起來很累人，我是說看起來很累的樣子。
泰伯：是啊！嗯！我們走了好長一段路。
茉莉：你們走了多遠呢？〔多久？〕
泰伯：大約 1 小時。
茉莉：啊？
泰伯：但是我們抓到了我們要追的那個人。
茉莉：是啊！局長會很高興的。
泰伯：你做得很好，王幹員。
茉莉：這要謝謝你才對，泰伯幹員。

EXAMPLES... EXAMPLES... EXAMPLES...

- I walked a long way. —— How far did you walk?
  我走了好長一段路。—— 你走了多遠？
- I walked a long time. —— How long did you walk?
  我走了好久。—— 你走了多久？
- How far is it to the next gas station? —— About a mile.
  到下個加油站有多遠？—— 大概 1 英里。
- How long is it since you had a holiday? —— It's two years.
  距你上次放假有多久了？—— 兩年了。

...NOTES ...NOTES ...NOTES

How 問句的後面加 long 表示詢問期間；far 表示詢問距離；soon 表示詢問時間快慢；often 則是詢問次數。

How soon does the next bus leave? —— In 20 minutes.
下一班公車還要多久才開？—— 20 分鐘內。

How often do you see him?
你多久見他一次？

75

這禮拜四有個會議。

There will be a meeting this Thursday.

Mike: Hello, Mari?

Mari: **Mike! How are you?**

Mike: Great! One more week and training is over.

Mari: **And we can get married.**

Mike: It's like a dream, isn't it?

Mari: **There will be a meeting** on this Thursday **to decide where we will work.**

Mike: The director knows we're getting married, so...

Mari: **I hope they keep us together.**

Mike: Don't worry.

Mari: **OK, Mike, I won't worry. See you *on next Sunday.**

Mike: I love you.

Mari: ***I also.**

*on next Sunday → next Sunday
*I also. → Me, too.

麥克：哈囉，茉莉嗎？
茉莉：麥克！你好嗎？
麥克：棒極了！再一個禮拜訓練就結束了。
茉莉：然後我們就可以結婚了。
麥克：就像在做夢一樣，不是嗎？
茉莉：這禮拜四有個會議，要決定我們未來的工作地點。
麥克：局長知道我們要結婚，所以……
茉莉：我希望他們把我們安排在一起。
麥克：別擔心。
茉莉：OK，麥克，我不擔心。下禮拜天見。
麥克：我愛你。
茉莉：我也是。

EXAMPLES... EXAMPLES... EXAMPLES...

- What are you doing this evening?
  你今晚要做什麼？
- Goodbye! See you next Monday!
  再見！下週一見！
- I'll be in the office every day next week except Monday.
  我下週除了星期一以外，每天都會在公司。
- We'll see you tomorrow afternoon.
  我們明天下午見。

...NOTES ...NOTES ...NOTES

以「this, next, last, one, every, each, some, any, all」開始的「時間說法」不用加上介系詞一起使用。

tomorrow morning, yesterday evening 等，同樣也不須用到介系詞。

76

可不可以請您說大聲一點?

Can you speak louder, please?

Foot: Hello? Agent Wang?

Mari: **Yes, that's me.**

Foot: This is Director Foot.

Mari: **Oh, hello, sir. Can I help you?**

Foot: I would like to come down and see you in your office.

Mari: ***Every time is OK, sir, but why?**

Foot: Well, I've heard about your good work.

Mari: **Oh, thank you, sir, but *I am nothing special woman.**

Foot: What was that, Agent Wang?

Mari: **Sorry? Can you speak loud please?**

Foot: Can I come down at around three, then?

Mari: **Can you come *early?**

Foot: I beg your pardon?

Mari: **Ye....yes sir, anything...time, sir.**

Foot: Jolly good then.

*Every time → Any time
*I am nothing special woman → it's nothing really
*early → earlier

孚特: 哈囉? 王幹員嗎?
茉莉: 是的, 我就是。
孚特: 我是孚特局長。
茉莉: 噢! 哈囉, 長官。需要我做什麼嗎?
孚特: 我想下去到你的辦公室見見你。
茉莉: 隨時都可以的, 長官。但是, 為什麼呢?
孚特: 嗯! 我聽說了你的優異表現。
茉莉: 噢! 謝謝您長官, 但是您太過獎了。
孚特: 那是什麼意思, 王幹員?
茉莉: 對不起您是說? 可不可以請您說大聲一點?
孚特: 那麼我 3 點下去可以嗎?
茉莉: 您可以早點來嗎? 〔早來嗎? 〕
孚特: 請再說一次?
茉莉: 是……是的長官, 任何事……時候都行, 長官。
孚特: 非常好, 到時見。

EXAMPLES... EXAMPLES... EXAMPLES...

- You're late. I expected you to be here earlier.
  你遲到了。我原本預期你會早點到。
- Could you speak more slowly, please?
  可以請你說慢一點嗎?
- You look thinner. Have you lost weight?
  你看來瘦了。你減輕體重了嗎?
- Let's go by car. It's much cheaper.
  我們坐車去吧! 這樣便宜多了。
- Can you be a bit quieter?
  你可以安靜點嗎?

...NOTES ...NOTES ...NOTES

表示「與～作比較」時, 必須用形容詞、副詞的比較級形式。

77

是嗎?

Was it?

Mari: **Hello? Mike?**

Mike: Mari! Hi! I was just about to call you.

Mari: **I called many times, but you were out.**

Mike: I had to attend an embassy party. I just got back.

Mari: **An embassy party? Wow!**

Mike: Oh, it was a terrible party.

Mari: Is it?

Mike: *Was it*, Mari.

Mari: **Oh, yes, of course. But why?**

Mike: Why what?

Mari: **.....uhhh**

茉莉: 哈囉? 麥克嗎?
麥克: 茉莉! 嗨! 我才正要打電話給你。
茉莉: 我打了好多次, 但你不在。
麥克: 我必須出席一場大使館的宴會。我剛剛回來的。
茉莉: 一場大使館的宴會? 哇!
麥克: 噢! 那是場糟透了的宴會。
茉莉: 是嗎?
麥克: Was it, 茉莉。
茉莉: 噢! 對, 當然。但是為什麼呢?
麥克: 什麼為什麼?
茉莉: 呃……

EXAMPLES... EXAMPLES... EXAMPLES...

- The exam was very difficult.—— Was it?
  考試非常的難。——是嗎?
- Mary came yesterday.—— Did she?
  瑪麗昨天回來了。——是嗎?
- She's not going to help you.—— Isn't she?
  她不會幫你的。——是嗎? / 她不會嗎?
- There'll be a strike soon.—— Will there?
  很快就會有場罷工。——是嗎? / 會有嗎?

...NOTES ...NOTES ...NOTES

表示「對對方的話感興趣」時, 可以利用對方的句型作成「助動詞 + 代名詞」的短問句形式作回應, 效果相當於 Really!「真的嗎」。

對方的句型如果是肯定句就用肯定問句, 如果是否定句就用否定問句。

表現的語意由聲調高低決定, 上昇聲調表示感興趣, 下降聲調表示怒意、不信任等。

78 我遲到了，是不是？

I'm late, aren't I?

Sue: Good morning, Agent Wang.

Mari: **You're the new secretary, aren't you?**

Sue: Ah, yes, that's me, Sue Lindon.

Mari: **Nice to meet you, Sue.**

Sue: It's my pleasure.

Mari: **Are there any messages for me?**

Sue: One from Director Foot.

Mari: **I forgot the meeting! I'm late,** amn't I?

Sue: You're lucky. The meeting was canceled.

Mari: ***Thank gods! Give me a hand, *do you?**

Sue: Ah, yes, of course. This is heavy!

Mari: **Don't look inside, it's a surprise.**

Sue: For who?

Mari: **For you! Let's have a party, *will you?**

Sue: A party for me?!

Mari: **Welcome to the CIA, Sue!**

*Thank gods! → Thank god!
*do you? → will you?
*will you? → shall we?

蘇：　早安，王幹員。
茉莉：你就是那個新來的秘書？
蘇：　喔！是的，就是我，蘇・林登。
茉莉：很高興認識你，蘇。
蘇：　這是我的榮幸。
茉莉：有沒有人留言給我？
蘇：　孚特局長來了一通。
茉莉：我忘了要開會了！我遲到了是不是？
蘇：　你很幸運。會議取消了。
茉莉：謝天謝地！幫我拿一下好嗎？
蘇：　噢！是的，當然。這東西好重喔！
茉莉：不可以看裡面，那是個驚喜。
蘇：　給誰的？
茉莉：給你的！我們來開派對吧！好不好呀？
蘇：　給我的派對？
茉莉：歡迎來到 CIA，蘇！

EXAMPLES... EXAMPLES... EXAMPLES...

- Open the door, will you?
  開一下門好嗎？
- Let's go for a walk, shall we?
  我們去散步吧！如何？
- We've met before, haven't we? —— Yes.
  我們以前見過，對吧？ —— 是的。
- We haven't met before, have we? —— No.
  我們以前沒見過，對吧？ —— 是的。

...NOTES ...NOTES ...NOTES

以短問句結尾的句子可以表示「徵求對方的同意」（下降聲調），或是「要求得到確認」（上昇聲調）。

希望得到 Yes 的回答時，就用「肯定句加否定問句」。反之，希望得到 No 的回答就用「否定句加肯定問句」的句型。

I'm..., aren't I? Let's..., shall we?和祈使句的用法較特別，需注意。

79 對不起，我可以借您的電話用用嗎？

Excuse me, can I use your phone?

任務進行途中，茱莉的行動電話出現斷訊

Mari: **Agent Tubs? (crackle, crackle), hello?**

Tubs: He...Agen....(crackle)....to the corn....

Mari: **Hello? What? I think we have a bad connection.**

Tubs: (Crackle, crackle) now....dangerou.....

Mari: **Oh, no! the batteries are dead!**

茱莉向正在講行動電話的行人走去

Mari: **Excuse me, can I borrow your phone?**

Man: What? Ah, well, actually no!

Mari: **I'm with the CIA. Official business.**

Man: Oh, well, in that case, I suppose it's OK.

Mari: **Thank you.**

茉莉：泰伯幹員？（劈啪，劈啪），哈囉？
泰伯：這兒……幹員……（劈啪）……到……角……
茉莉：哈囉？什麼？我想我們的通訊不良。
泰伯：（劈啪，劈啪）現在……危險……
茉莉：噢！不！電池沒電了！

× × ×

茉莉：對不起，我可以借您的電話用用嗎？〔借走您的電話〕
男子：什麼？喔！嗯！老實說不行！
茉莉：我在 CIA 工作，這是公事。
男子：噢！好，如果是那樣的話，我想是可以的。
茉莉：謝謝。

EXAMPLES... EXAMPLES... EXAMPLES...

- Does she usually wear spectacles?(× put on)
  她通常都戴眼鏡嗎？
- Tom likes to watch baseball game.(× look at)
  湯姆喜歡看棒球。
- I tried hard to listen to what he said.(× hear)
  我努力試著去聽懂他所說的。
- Have you taken your medicine yet?(× eat)
  你吃藥了沒有？
- I cut a class today.(× escaped from)
  我今天蹺課。

...NOTES ...NOTES ...NOTES

有些動詞雖然意思相近，但是用法不同。例如同樣是「穿」，put on 表示的是「穿戴上～」（動作），而 wear 則是「穿戴著～」（狀態）。這類動詞其他還有 watch「注視（動態物體）」和 look at「注視（靜物）」，hear「（不經意）聽見、聽到」和 listen to「聆聽」等。

borrow 的意思是指「將所借物品帶走」，如果只是當場暫時借用，一般都是用 use。

80

愈是危險我愈喜歡。

The more dangerous it is, the more I like it.

Mike: Well, Mari, we're finally husband and wife.

Mari: **Yes, Mike. Our dreams have come true.**

Mike: Well, when are you going to quit?

Mari: **What?! What do you mean, Mike?**

Mike: Well, I thought a good Chinese wife stayed at home and waited for her husband.

Mari: **Mike! That's very old-fashioned!**

Mike: But isn't this life a little dangerous for you?

Mari: The more **it is** dangerous, **the more *I like.**

Mike: But who's going to make dinner every evening?

Mari: **I can't believe this!**

Mike: Well, not tomorrow, but....

Mari: **Mike, we have to talk.**

To be continued...

*I like → I like it

麥克：好了，茉莉，我們總算成為夫妻了。
茉莉：是呀！麥克。我們的夢想成真了。
麥克：嗯！你打算什麼時候辭職？
茉莉：什麼？！你是什麼意思，麥克？
麥克：嗯！我以為一個好的中國太太是待在家裡，等她先生的呀！
茉莉：麥克！那早就過時啦！
麥克：可是這種生活對你而言不會稍嫌危險嗎？
茉莉：愈是危險我愈喜歡。
麥克：可是誰來煮每天的晚餐呢？
茉莉：我真是不敢相信！
麥克：嗯！不是要你明天就……
茉莉：麥克，我們必須談談。

EXAMPLES... EXAMPLES... EXAMPLES...

- The harder you work, the more successful you will be.
  你工作愈認真，就會愈成功。
- The more I got to know him, the more I liked him.
  我愈了解他，就愈喜歡他。
- The more electricity you use, the higher your bill will be.
  你用愈多的電，你的帳單就會愈貴。

...NOTES ...NOTES ...NOTES

「the + 比較級～， the + 比較級……」的意思是「愈～，就愈……」，放在形容詞或副詞等的比較級之前的 the，不可以省略。

有時為了求簡潔，除「the + 比較級」的部分外，均可考慮加以刪除。

What time shall we leave? —— The sooner the better.
我們何時離開？ —— 愈快愈好。

後　記

Our life is one big story, but within that larger story, we all have a story of our own. And that story should be told. Every story has a meaning and something to teach the rest of us. That is, if we can read between the lines to find that meaning.

We have tried to make the whole question of what is or is not grammatically correct more human and more approachable. The story of Mari could be the story of any one of us as we venture out beyond our own familiar world into a new one. Perhaps the biggest lesson to be learned from Mari is her readiness to try anything and to keep making mistakes until she gets it right. There is no shame in making mistakes when speaking a foreign language. It is rather a shame that more people do not make more mistakes instead of wondering and pondering over deep philosophical and grammatical questions of grave importance and consequence.

Grammar lays down certain guidelines and rules to facilitate communication in any given language. When grammar itself becomes a hindrance to communication, then it loses its meaning and purpose.

We have tried to show here that even though you may be making a grammatical mistake, more often than not, what you are trying to get across does indeed get across. And that is more important than anything else. We have the gift of speech, and though there are countless languages spoken throughout the world, the need and desire to speak to others seems to be a universal trait.

Many of the mistakes that Mari makes stem from her habit of translating directly from Chinese into English. This will almost always come out wrong, as a language is a reflection of a long history and culture that is necessarily different from your own.

So it is pointless to ask the question,「『相親』用英語或是其他外語要怎麼說？」 as such a custom may not exist there. Why not think in terms of,「外國是不是也有經由親友介紹結婚的說法？」 This is a much more global way of thinking, and if you can learn to think in this way, your own language learning will surely take a leap forward.

So go out and start writing your own story. It's as simple as opening your mouth and starting to speak. The grammar will follow after you.

Miguel Rivas-Micoud

一板一眼的「文法」就算錯了又何妨，在第 25 單元裡 John 不是說了嗎！ You have to make mistakes to improve.

你是不是已經準備好要迎接另一個更不一樣的大膽妹——茉莉了呢？現在筆者就要把這個任務交給你，希望每個和茉莉的冒險一路走來的讀者，都能自己在生活中譜寫出屬於自己的未完成的故事。加油！

大 石 健

國家圖書館出版品預行編目資料

MAD茉莉的文法冒險／大石 健，
Miguel Rivas-Micoud著；三民
書局編輯部譯，--初版．--臺北市：
三民，民88
面； 公分
ISBN 957-14-2920-1（平裝）

1. 英國語言-文法

805.16 87014656

網際網路位址 http://www.sanmin.com.tw

© MAD茉莉的文法冒險

著作人 大石 健 Miguel Rivas-Micoud
譯 者 三民書局編輯部
發行人 劉振强
著作財產權人 三民書局股份有限公司
臺北市復興北路三八六號
發行所 三民書局股份有限公司
地 址／臺北市復興北路三八六號
電 話／二五〇〇六六〇〇
郵 撥／〇〇〇九九九八——五號
印刷所 三民書局股份有限公司
門市部 復北店／臺北市復興北路三八六號
重南店／臺北市重慶南路一段六十一號
初 版 中華民國八十八年一月
編 號 S 80210
基本定價 叁元捌角
行政院新聞局登記證局版臺業字第〇二〇〇號

ISBN 957-14-2920-1（平裝）